The Islands of Rune

by Maria Levato

DORRANCE PUBLISHING CO

EST. 1920

PITTSBURGH, PENNSYLVANIA 15238

Dorrance Publishing Co
585 Alpha Drive
Suite 103
Pittsburgh, PA 15238
Visit our website at *www.dorrancebookstore.com*

ISBN: 979-8-8868-3077-4
eISBN: 979-8-8868-3937-1

1

In a world much different from the one you know today, a world of ancient ways and the most fascinating of skill sets, there lies the land of Loft. Loft used to be an average kingdom. At the time they held no magic and because of that, the people of Loft were almost dangerously unaware of the truth about the world they lived in. Just a few miles off the coast was a group of five islands. These islands were called the Islands of Rune. They were beautiful and full of magical runes but hidden well beyond a cloud bank that never left. It protected the people of the islands from the people of the mainland so that mainlanders would never find out the truth about the islanders. Both the mainland of Loft and the islands had been riddled with many injustices, that is until one man decided to make a difference.

Today, I tell the story of what happened all those years ago for the first time. In my old age, I have come to fear that if the histories of our lands are not passed on, future generations will come to repeat the mistakes of our past. Of course, hiding the truths of the world is how things got so messed up to begin with, so it makes sense I would feel this way. Therefore, I am writing this to document the truth of what occurred when the team now known as "The Inter-Kingdom Board of Peace and Foreign Relations" was formed.

In truth, we started out as a group of kids with an impossible dream and a boat. I was about nineteen at the time. As most of you reading this will know, I was highborn. My father was first cousin to the Queen of Loft, his title was Duke, and I was the heiress to the title of Duchess. I was a spoiled child who had little regard for those beneath my station. However, I was still kinder than my parents in that sense. I suppose it did not help that my mother and father were who they were, they made me believe that my behavior was normal. They also saw being kindhearted or caring as a flaw. They were also not the nicest people I have ever known; I honestly cannot say if they meant harm by what they did or if they were just ignorant to the harm they caused because of the world they knew. It is not my place to judge whether harm was intended. Regardless, I did come to find that no matter one's intentions, if harm if being done, it is my place to stop it. That, my friends, is everyone's place. Perhaps my biggest regret is never having an honest conversation with them.

The beginning of this story goes back to a single moment, on a day that changed my life. I was walking through town when I met him for the first time. I remember it like it was yesterday. I was young and my views about the world were so limited, my biggest concern was figuring out how to get out of the engagement my parents were trying to force me into. I begged and pleaded with my mother as she dragged me through town to prepare me for the meeting with this suitor.

"But, Mama, I do not want to wed yet. I want to wait until a man can offer me something more than this life. I want passion, adventure, love, and fun."

"Oh, you ridiculous girl." She rolled her eyes. "It is time that you grow up and stop believing in those stories. You are of age and it is past time you wed. The Prince of Rallem is a great match and a marriage to him will increase our family's status and fortune tenfold. I will not hear anything more about it. If you do anything to spoil this, I will make your life a living hell. You will be disinherited and locked in a dungeon for the rest of your days."

I gulped, realizing the seriousness of my mother's threat. I was silent after that, yet my mind was anything but. I knew I could not marry this man as my mother wished me to. If I went with her today, I would be married off within a months' time. While my family is important to me, they already had status and wealth, they need not have any more of it. I did not have happiness, adventure, and love. I owed it to myself to find such things.

I took a deep breath and decided that my only choice was to run. I knew my parents would come searching for me, but I had to do what I could to escape this fate. While my mother was talking to a shopkeeper, I snuck out the door. I had no clue where I was heading, but I knew I had to leave Loft. My mother and father were too powerful. If I remained here, I would surely be caught. I ran towards the docks hoping I could buy passage onto a ship with what gold I had on me, but I knew I had to be careful whose ship I boarded.

When I arrived at the docks, I looked around, and I saw a lone man preparing a ship. I approached him and cleared my throat to gain his attention. "This is quite a large ship to be manning alone, is it not?"

He smiled, looking down at me from aboard the ship. "I manage. Why do you ask?"

"No reason, I was just looking for passage aboard one of these ships. I do have gold, but I thought that I may be able to work for my passage on a ship as ill-manned as yours, allowing me to keep my gold."

"Can you cook? I would not mind having a cook aboard. I survive, but I cannot say anything I make is to my liking."

I nodded.

"Very well then, climb aboard."

I did, but I kept my distance from him. His name was Malachi. He was a shorter man with big, bulky muscles. His skin was dark and he had short hair, but it was wild. He looked as if he spent most of his time on this ship. I figured him for a merchant at first. I was curious about the strange markings that covered his arms and chest. I had never seen anything like them before.

Shortly after I boarded the ship, I noticed Malachi talking to some men, they looked like guards. I realized I may have caused trouble for him as they began to search the ship, pinning Malachi to the ground. I stepped out of my cabin and demanded that they release him, explaining that I was not kidnapped, that I had run away from my parents and that I had no intention of returning. The guards insisted that I had no choice in the matter as they attempted to drag me off the ship, but Malachi suddenly summoned these balls of fire to his hands and said, "Release the girl now or I will destroy you."

The guards and I were all amazed at what we were seeing, such power was unheard of in Loft. However, the guards tried to regain their composure, insisting that Malachi would not launch an attack because he would risk hitting me.

Malachi replied, "I know my own skill level. I will not hit the girl. This is your last chance to release her."

The guards called his bluff, but that turned out to be a mistake on their part. Malachi defeated them swiftly and threw them off the ship. We left the dock and set sail immediately after, knowing that more guards would be coming after us if we did not. At that moment, I felt like I would never return to Loft again.

After we were a safe distance from the docks, I asked Malachi, "Why did you help me?"

"You were going to turn yourself in to protect me. It is obvious that you are a good person who is in a bad situation."

"Well, it was not fair for them to treat you that way. You did not know who I was."

"To be fair, I am also not stupid. Look at how you are dressed. The fine red silks, the fancy hairdo, those shoes look brand new. You are clearly a high-ranking noble girl; anyone could tell from one look at you. You should get changed. Those clothes will get ruined on this ship."

I was going to do as he asked, but first I wanted to know who he was. So, I asked him. He explained, "I am from the Fire Island of Rune, Tendu. The Islands possess magical runes that its natives can harness power from. I am on a mission to build a team, one that will help people. I think I want you to be a part of that team if you want to be. I will also need one representative from each island, right now, I am heading to Pallentine."

I thought for a moment, then nodded. "Yes, I do!"

With that, our journey had begun. I was nervous, but excited still. So much had happened to me in that day it was hard to wrap my head around. I thought it best to get some sleep and try to start fresh tomorrow. Before I did, I sat down with Malachi and insisted that we make a toast.

"Why?" he asked.

"The start of our new friendship and our new team. Is that not worth toasting?"

He chuckled. "It sure is. To friendship and teamwork!"

"To friendship and teamwork!"

After that, I went to sleep. When I awoke our journey was well underway. It was exciting to think that I was going to the Islands of Rune. It has been said that no mainlander has ever been to the islands before; it is forbidden. Malachi had told me it is because the islanders do not want us knowing about their powers. He also told me a little about Pallentine. They use something called "nature-language runes." These runes allow them to communicate with nature, whether it be plants, the ocean, wind, or anything else in nature, including animals. I cannot help but wonder how such a skill is used. Apparently, they are also a warrior people who are unparalleled in hand-to-hand combat.

The Pallentinian Chief also has the gift of sight. His prophecies are said to be indisputable. Also, every time one departs his homeland, it is tradition that he gives them a prophecy to help guide them on their journey. I hoped I would get one, little did I know that the prophecy the Chief would give me was one that would haunt me for years to come.

That day came and went as well, and soon, it was time for me to prepare dinner. Malachi had limited supplies available on the ship, so I had to make do. I found it hard to believe that he lived like this all the time, but I suppose that I would have to get used to it. It was an adjustment from being a noble. I just hoped I had made the right decision. Marrying that man could not have been the right one. Who would want to be forced into a marriage with a man they do not know, let alone love? I know women do it all the time, but I am not just "women;" I am me. Perhaps I needed more than the life of just any woman. It was like I was programmed differently. All I know is that I had to try to find something more, something better. Is that really all that bad?

Malachi and I bonded during dinner. As it turned out, he was a nice guy. I enjoyed talking to him and learning more about him. He seemed like he wore his heart on his sleeve a lot; I liked that about him. Something about him gave me an off vibe, as if there was something lurking beneath the surface of this kind, gentle guy that no one would ever suspect. I did not feel threatened by it, perhaps just worried about Malachi. I hoped that he was all right. I knew that one day he would open up to me about it. It was just a matter of time. After all, we were still getting comfortable with one another. I would just have to be there to support him when he was ready.

2

It was later that night when the seas began to roar. I woke up from my sleep, screaming, and Malachi rushed to my cabin.

"Josie! Are you all right?"

I was scared, but I tried to hide it. "Y-yes, of course. I-I was j-just a bit startled." I stuttered as I shivered underneath the comforter. I had feared thunderstorms ever since I was a young girl. My father and mother were gone a lot, attending to affairs of state as the Duke and Duchess, and I often had to brave them alone. The maids and guards were always too busy working around the house to help me deal with my childish fears, so I guess I never got over it. Not that I do not understand why they were so busy; my mother and father have always been strict with the help. They once fired a maid for getting sick one time in the two decades she had worked in our home. They also spread the word that she was unreliable and made it impossible for her to find work with another family in Loft. I have no clue what became of her after that.

Malachi laughed, bringing my mind back to the conversation at hand. "It is okay. My ship has braved much worse waters than these before. Do not worry your pretty little head for a moment. Even if anything did happen, I am up steering the ship personally, so I would manage it."

I stopped shaking as I got distracted by what he said. "You are out there in the rain? But you will freeze? And you will never get any rest that way."

"It is okay, I am used to it. I can go a few days without sleep. I just want to be sure you can rest, okay?"

"No," I said passionately, "absolutely not okay! I will stay up with you and help you. I will not be a burden, nor will I allow you to overwork yourself in such a way. You are a person, not a mule, for Christ's sake."

I thought to myself, that I did not want to be like my parents. I wanted to be useful to Malachi. I did not want to treat him, or anyone for that matter, badly. I wanted to carry my weight and be a good person. Malachi had been so nice to me. I refused to continue to sit around acting like the entitled little noble girl I was raised to be.

He looked astonished. "You get so enthusiastic; how could I say no? Still, it seems a bit unnecessary. Come on, then, if you insist. It is about time I show you how I stay warm."

Confused, I asked him, "Malachi, what do you mean?"

"Just come on." He waved.

I followed him to the deck where he showed me the most amazing thing. He had me stand to the side and chanted, "Rune of runes, I call to you. Show your flames to me." Then, markings appeared all up his arms and he began to move his hands in beautiful, ritualistic patterns. The fire wrapped itself around me, but it did not burn; it just warmed me. He told me they were called flames of friendship and that fire did not have to burn.

I asked him, "You truly are gifted, Malachi. This is amazing. Is everyone on Tendu this skilled?"

"Well, all islanders have the power to harness the runes, sure. But we are not all granted equal strength by the runes by any means. I am by far one of the most skilled fire rune users Tendu has to offer, in fact, I am one of the most skilled rune users in all the five islands. However, be careful not to mistake powerful for gifted, Josie. Here, have a look at this. This rune right here is called Sowelo, it means 'poetic justice, energy, or the sun.' This one here is called Othila, it means 'authority, responsibility, inheritance, or loyalty.' Lastly, this one, Madr, it means 'mankind' or 'judgment.' Together, these runes tell my story. I inherited great authority, as well as great responsibility. Now, with the energy of the sun, otherwise called fire, I seek to deliver a poetic justice. However, one day, mankind will pass judgment on me for what I am. This power of mine is a curse that lies deep in my blood. Make no mistake, I would rid myself of it in a heartbeat if given the opportunity."

"Do not say such things, Malachi. It is that same power that grants you the ability to help others the way you wish to, without it, this 'team' you are trying to build would be hallow. No one would put their faith in those they believed to be weak. It is far from a curse to be able to protect those in need. I wish I could learn such a skill."

He looked surprised. "You are right. I should not complain. I have been given a great blessing in that aspect. You know, there is something about you that I just cannot explain? It is as if you hold a power that goes beyond the runes, something in your spirit. Perhaps you are more skilled than you realize."

"Thank you, Malachi." I smiled, but I was disappointed. I did not feel this power he spoke of; in truth, I felt weak. I had just runaway out of fear, too weak to face my parents down and standup for myself and sailed away in the care of some random man who rescued me. I could tell that he was in pain still. Whatever this "curse" he spoke of… it must genuinely take a toll on him. I worried about him. "You are far stronger than I, trust that."

Then, Malachi hollered, distracted by something he saw from a distance. "Look, Josie! We are here! That's Pallentine!"

Excited, I stood up and ran to the edge of the ship without thinking, I slipped and fell over the edge. Malachi yelled out. "Josie!"

I tried desperately to keep my head above water until Malachi could throw me a rope, but the waters were so wild, I kept getting pulled under. Malachi frantically searched for me so he knew where to throw the line but could not see me. I continued to struggle, gasping for what little air I could, but it was no use. The mighty sea was going to swallow me whole, but suddenly, a short, muscular woman on the shore touched the ground and chanted something quietly, causing sand to gather beneath me and carry me to shore, then disperse.

After catching my breath, I sat up and said to her. "Thank you. My name is Josie. My friend on the boat is Malachi. I am sure he will get here in a few minutes."

"Nice to meet you, Josie," the woman said to me. "My name is Johanna. You are not from the islands, are you? Oh, and please do not thank me. I simply asked him to save you."

I had no clue who she had asked to save me, I just knew I was thankful to him and her. I moved on, since I did not want to come across rude. "No. How could you tell I am not an islander so easily?"

"Most people from the islands don't think well of my people, we are too different for them."

"Well, I think that being different is a good thing," I told her. "And my friend, he is from Tendu, but he does too. We came here in hopes of befriending your people and finding one of you to represent your people on our team. We want to change injustices like the ones your people suffer and help those in need."

"That sounds interesting. You will have to tell the Chief all about it at the party, I am sure he will be most interested."

"Sounds good!"

Then Malachi came over. "Josie, oh my God, are you okay? You scared the life out of me."

I answered, "I am perfectly fine, Malachi. Thanks for the concern, though. This is Johanna. She has invited us to a party tonight where we can meet with the Chief and tell him of our plans. She thinks he will be interested. Also, I think we should suggest Johanna as the representative to the Chief. I like her."

Malachi laughed. "You liking someone is reason enough to choose them?"

"I am trusting my instincts. It is how you chose me, is it not? It is all the reason I need."

"Yes, of course. You have a point. Thanks for saving her, Johanna. I think you would be a great candidate for the representative too. Josie's reasoning would not have worked in any logical mind, but I trust her instincts whole-heartedly. I have a good feeling about it if she does."

Johanna laughed. "You guys are weird, I like it. I would be up for tagging along. Although, I must admit I am totally confused about how this was decided. But the Chief might want to choose someone a bit more up to the task. I am just border patrol, not a diplomat."

I smiled. "That makes you perfect for this mission. We do not need a bunch of statesmen and what not. We need regular people who just so happen to care about other people, most people do not realize this, but having a good heart is a skill set in and of itself."

Johanna nodded, then led the way to the village. Upon arrival, she told us, "We all live in this village. Do not wander off alone because you will get lost, only natives can navigate this land. We can relax at my house until the party, I am sure you have had a long journey. I live alone, so we will not be bothered."

At her house, I took a shower and got some rest. It was nice after being on that boat all day. Malachi showered too, then rested a bit. I woke up before him, so I talked to Johanna for a bit. She asked, "So, are you and Malachi together?"

I hesitated. "Like, in a romantic sense? Oh God, no. We are just friends. He is a great guy and I must admit he is not bad-looking, but I cannot see us that way. He is more like a brother. In a romantic sense, I would want someone with more fire in their personality. He is so stereotypically perfect it's annoying in a way."

"Good, because now I can admit I think he's cute."

I laughed. "You should go for it, then."

"You think so? I am not too masculine for him?"

"Well, I do not know what his taste in women is like. But I do not think he is that superficial. Plus, you may be muscular, but you are not masculine. You just look like an athletic, strong woman. You are beautiful and well-toned. I am so jealous of your long hair too. Mine will never grow past my shoulders."

"But it is cute that way! And so curly! You have pretty, deep blue eyes too. They are gorgeous. Plus, you have that tall, slender frame, that almost any man will go for."

I guess Malachi had woken up because he suddenly butted in, "You are both remarkable, radiant women who I admire greatly. Neither of you better let me hear you say anything negative about yourselves, understood?"

We both laughed and said, "Yes, Malachi." Simultaneously as we pressed our faces together and smiled.

Then, I asked Johanna to tell me about her runes too. Hers were Ur, for ferocity, Tyr, for binding agreements or commitment, and Ehwaz, for ideas, adventure, and the animal world. It was cool hearing about the runes and the powers they gave to the islanders. I wondered what other intriguing runes we would come across in our travels. As for Johanna, it was odd. I had only just meant her, but somehow, we were already in sync. I already felt that she was special to me. I have never had many friends before, but I imagined this was what having a best friend would feel like. It is like we just went together in a way that made no sense, only the two of us could ever understand it, and it could not be described in something as simple as words.

We all got ready to head to the village party. Excited to meet the Chief, I asked Johanna what we should be expecting on the way there. She told me it is all rather informal. I was relieved it would not be nervous like it was on the mainland; I had always hated those stuffy events. Once we arrived at the party, we danced and listened to music. The food and drinks were great too. Johanna took us to meet the Chief toward the end of the night.

He greeted us. "Hello, friends. Johanna has told me you are nice and interesting people. Please share with me these plans of yours."

Malachi replied, "Yes, well, in short, we are going to change the world. Your people are discriminated against because people from the other islands have not tried at understanding the culture of this land. On my island, Tendu, people are dying from starvation and disease because those in power feed off us. The north of Nollent oppresses the south leaving brother torn from brother and sister torn from sister due to an imaginary line on their island. Oceanica and Tendu have been trying to murder each other for centuries. Since the Renugi family stole the throne from the Renki, far too many have died senselessly. The mainland is painfully unaware of everything that is going on. Something needs to give; it needs to change. And I intend to change it. I will gather a team of individuals, one person to represent each place, and we will resolve this. From the mainland, I have Josie, whose heart is made of gold.

From Pallentine, I ask that you send Johanna, as she is not only powerful but has displayed an unbelievable ability to create friendships and trust from the simplest of situations."

The Chief nodded. "I do not disagree with you about what is necessary. This world is plagued with many injustices, some of which my people have become targets of. It causes me great pain to see the hatred that fills the hearts of men. I want to be a part of this team you speak of, one that aims to become a solution rather than another problem. However, you will need to prove to me that you and Josie are capable of the task at hand prior to me giving my consent for Johanna to leave with you. Her parents died when she was just a girl and I have raised her as my own, as I have with all the orphans of this great island, we call our home. I will not let my daughter leave with strangers on such a dangerous mission if they cannot prove themselves capable and trustworthy."

Malachi looked at me and I gave him a nod, then turned back to the Chief and said, "Let's do it."

The Chief smiled. "Very well then. You and the woman will be taken to the most remote corner of the island. If in three days' time you have returned to us, Johanna will leave with you. If not, we will retrieve you and return you to your ship, but Johanna will stay."

We nodded and with that, we began to prepare. We had an hour to do so. Malachi rushed to grab some essentials; then he looked at me and said, "Josie, I need you to listen to me very carefully. First and foremost, if at any point this is too hard for you, tell me and we will forfeit. Second, if anything happens to me, promise me you will leave me. Third, you absolutely must always stay by my side, no more than five steps away. Lastly, do not touch, eat, drink, or do anything that I do not expressly tell you is okay. Do you understand?"

I nodded, then looked down out of fear that I would be deadweight to Malachi. After we finished, the natives blindfolded us and took us to our starting point. We took off the blindfolds, then the natives ran off, disappearing into the forest in all different directions to confuse us further. The trial had begun. I immediately felt disoriented by the lack of direction; it made me feel sick to my stomach.

Although I was nervous going into it, I felt reassured having Malachi with me. Somehow, I knew that we would be just fine. Strange noises came from every direction, and from the looks of it, every animal in the vicinity was staring at us. I did not know what to do first. However, as I was standing there paralyzed in my fear, Malachi was planning. He suddenly spoke, bringing me back out of my overwhelming thoughts, "Josie, come on. We are going this way."

I nodded, but as I began to walk, I heard something telling me not to go that way. I looked around, unsure of where the voice was coming from, and then a little fox jumped up on my shoulder and said again, "You really shouldn't go that way."

I said, "Hey Malachi, I don't think we should go that way."

"What? What are you talking about?" He turned and looked at me.

I replied, "This fox, it told me we should not go that way. I think we should listen to it. Something in me is telling me to trust her. I must say, it is strange, though. I have never spoken to an animal before."

He said, "That is not a normal fox, Josie, that is a spirit fox. You probably never met a spirit animal before either. They do not typically choose to live on the mainland, especially not Loft. Wild ones live here in bulk, though. There is plenty of spiritual energy for them here. Can you really talk to it?"

I said to the fox, "We need to show him that we can communicate. Jump for me."

The fox jumped.

"Now climb that tree."

The fox climbed onto a branch.

"Now come back over here."

The fox sat back on my shoulder.

Malachi's jaw dropped. "How did you do that? Josie, you have a gift. Ask it to guide us. That is not something just anyone can do. In fact, I have never met anyone who can speak to spirit animals before."

So, I asked the fox and she agreed. Her name was Kimble. She guided us through the trees and such. This journey would still be dangerous, but thanks to Kimble, we had a decent chance. Malachi gathered food and water where he could. I learned a lot about navigating the island, which plants were safe and which were dangerous, and how to find water and shelter in the wild. It was very exciting, though I must admit, it took some adjusting. We were about a day and a half into our trip when Kimble said to me, "The trip is going to become more dangerous from here on out. You should tell that man to arm himself just in case."

I gave her a nod and said to him, "Malachi, Kimble said the trip is going to get more dangerous and you should stay armed from here on out."

Malachi nodded, then began to concentrate, raising bloodred flames into his palms. He explained to me, "Josie, these are called the flames of hell. Only descendants of Tendu's first royal family can raise them from the power of the runes. I am technically a prince by blood. As you will recall, my family, the Renki was toppled generations after we established the Tendu we know today and the family that took over, the Renugi family, has varied greatly from the original vision for Tendu, and because of that our land and our people are dying. I feel it is my responsibility to fix it because it is my land by birthright."

I smiled at him and nodded. He really did have a prince's heart. Without even realizing it, Malachi had gained my full faith in him. I genuinely did believe he could change the world; it was then I knew the team he was creating would do great things. He was not just some kindhearted peasant boy with dreams larger than he was; he was a good man with a noble heart and the power to do anything he set his mind to. His goal was completely realistic. I admired him. My goals were all so selfish, love, happiness, adventure…. I was nothing more than a little girl, spoiled and superficial. I felt disappointed in myself.

Malachi suddenly interrupted my thoughts, saying, "Josie, I am going to need you to stop doing that. Every time that looks is on your face, I can tell you do not see your own value. Your heart is even purer than my own. You are by far the most valuable member of this team I am creating; without you, it is not possible. There is a lot you do not realize about yourself yet, but trust me, you are invaluable."

I smiled at him half-heartedly and nodded, but I still could not see what he saw. "I guess I will have to take your word for it, for now. Thank you, Malachi."

He nodded back.

Kimble then said to me, "You should not think about yourself that way, Josie. You are my friend and I like you. Don't you know what that means?"

"No, what does it mean?"

Kimble explained, "You cannot talk to other animals or nature like a Pallentinian, but a Pallentinian also could not talk to me. Those with very pure hearts can sometimes cause spirit animals like me to become attracted to them, allowing us to communicate. I believe humans call the phenomenon having a familiar. Yes, that is it. I am your familiar and foxes, like myself, are known for being the most powerful of familiars. Thus, we are available only to those who have the greatest potential. Your spiritual power is immaculate. For me, regular spiritual energy is like mud. It slows me down and makes me feel sluggish, yet it keeps me alive. Yours is like water with not a single impurity; not only does drinking it keep me alive, but it also makes me energetic and happy."

I was amazed. "Wow! How did I gain such power?"

Kimble laughed. "Well, my guess is that it has to do with your lineage. Based on your scent, you are the great-great-granddaughter of the Priestess Linola, who singlehandedly protected Loft in the last war. You did not know that?"

I shook my head. "I had no clue that war even occurred. I think most people on the mainland are unaware of it. I wonder why. What good does it do to erase the past? It can only lead to us repeating mistakes. We cannot learn from mistakes we do not remember making."

Kimble agreed. "That is correct. Unfortunately, I fear it may be too late. The material world has begun to feel much like it did prior to the last war. I can feel the land's anger beginning to swell."

"No, we must stop it!" I said, "We must do something in time. I will not allow our ignorance to destroy us." As I got exceedingly upset, white lights began to shoot out from my body and I began to levitate.

Malachi and Kimble called out, "Josie!"

Malachi continued, "Josie, you have to calm down. You do not have control over your power yet, you could destroy the entire island. Just breathe, I promise you, we will not allow it to come to that."

Malachi's words resonated with me and I collapsed to the ground. I was completely drained of energy, but I was fine otherwise. However, it seemed that my fit brought us some unwanted attention. Suddenly, a rock came flying at Malachi from behind. He lifted me and jumped out of the way. He looked around, trying to find our attacker, but it was nowhere to be seen. More rocks came flying, but Malachi dodged them with me in his arms and Kimble on his shoulder. There was one he could not dodge. It hit us head-on. The impact sent me flying into the trunk of a nearby tree; I was unconscious for the rest of the fight.

When I woke, we were in a cave and Kimble was licking my face. I sat up and Malachi turned around from messing with the campfire. "Hey, you are awake. How are you feeling?"

"Ugh! I am okay, just a bit of a headache. What happened?"

Malachi explained, "We were attacked by a giant ape. I guess we stumbled into its territory. They are peaceful creatures if you respect them, but when they feel disrespected, they can be vicious. But I was able to take care of it, so there is no need to worry anymore."

I gasped. "Malachi! You did not kill that poor creature, did you?"

Malachi laughed. "Of course not, Josie. I just knocked it unconscious long enough to get us somewhere safe. I am not a monster."

I sighed in relief. "Good." Then I asked Kimble, "How far off are we from the village?"

Kimble contemplated for a moment. "I think we can get there by tomorrow afternoon if all goes as planned. We do have to leave early tomorrow to do it. We only have a one-hour span when it is safe to cross the valley."

I nodded, then told Malachi we should leave early tomorrow. He agreed; then we all got some rest. It was a well-deserved rest after a long day, but it was still hard to sleep. There were bugs biting and it was hot and humid. We were also on the ground so it was not comfortable to lie down. Nevertheless, it was all the rest we could get.

3

The following day, I woke up before Malachi, which was a rare occurrence. Kimble had woken me. I went over to him and gently woke him, saying, "Malachi, we should pack up and get moving."

He awoke with a smile on his face. "Mmm, I guess we should. I am getting up. Can you start getting everything together for me?"

I nodded then started packing, Malachi seemed extremely famished. That fight must have taken a lot out of him. I was kind of worried about him. Shortly after, the packing was done and we started to head out. Kimble led us down a rocky path that led to a valley the natives called The Valley of the Lost. It was a strange and dangerous valley filled with demonic energy where no plant would grow. As a matter of fact, the energy was so tainted, Kimble said it made her feel nauseous. Malachi and Kimble both warned me that crossing the valley was particularly dangerous for those who are pure of heart because the demons who linger there try to consume the souls of the pure.

Of course, that made me nervous because as much as he tried to hide it, Malachi was weakened badly and I did not know how to use whatever spiritual power I did have properly. I figured I just had to have faith that if Malachi said he could protect me, he could. And so, we began to cross the Valley of the Lost. Upon entering the valley, even I could feel the dark energy around us. Kimble was right, it was sickening. Kimble guided us step-by-step through the valley when suddenly, Malachi collapsed. The evil energy had drained what little strength he had left. I tried to carry him, but I could not. I could hear him mumbling. It sounded like he was telling me to leave him, but I could not, regardless of the promise I had made to him back in the village.

I sat by his side desperately trying to lift his body when Kimble said to me, "Physically, you do not have the strength to lift him."

I scoffed. "And what? Spiritually, I do? That is great and all, but I have no clue how to use my power. I have not any training. Can you give me instructions?"

"My dear Josie, it is not something that can be taught anyhow. You must be strong for Malachi now. You must have faith in yourself."

I closed my eyes and tried to listen to my heart. When I did, it was as if the world around me came to a halt. Everything was silent, I felt no movement or fear, it was just me, and at that moment, my strength was needed. I heard a peaceful melody with someone chanting to it, but I could not tell who and I could not make out what they were saying. I called out to them in my soul, asking them to help me. Then, I saw it. It was Kimble's true spirit, a large fox spirit residing in the spirit realm. The Kimble with me physically was just a part of Kimble's spirit that she sent to be with me. I asked her to help me and she chanted those words again. But this time, I heard her clearly. I realized she wanted me to chant with her, so I began chanting.

"Kimble, I call on you. Come to me and you will be free."

After three times, Kimble was freed from the spirit world and materialized in front of me. She was the most beautiful thing I had ever seen. She said, "Josie, thank you for freeing me. It has been nearly one thousand years since I have roamed the material world. Please, feel free to ask me for anything. Us fox spirits are very loyal familiars."

I smiled. "Kimble, you are far more than my familiar, you are my friend. Now let us get going."

I struggled to lift Malachi onto Kimble's back and then climbed on myself. Then, Kimble began to run. She said to me, "Hold on tight, Josie, we have to hurry. But I will have you back to the village in no time. Malachi will be so happy when he wakes up."

"Yes, he will be. I am glad you are here, Kimble. Out of curiosity, will stay with me when I leave this island?"

Kimble laughed. "Josie, my place is wherever you are. It was my choice to serve you. I could have chosen anyone. Even a dimwit would take me as a partner, surely even they would recognize that I am far more powerful than most familiars. I am more powerful than most foxes, honestly. You were a conscious choice, not a forced one. If you leave, me staying here is pointless. And trust me, the spirit world is not the type of place you spend time willingly. I want to stay with you and help you, that is if you want me to?"

"Of course, I do Kimble, thank you." Then, I pet her neck.

We continued to run for quite some time when I heard Malachi begin to wake. I looked down at him. "Malachi, how are you feeling?"

He was still out of it, but he replied, "Uhm, I am fine. Where are we?"

I explained, "We are riding Kimble. She's taking us to the village."

Confused, he sat up and began to look around. He asked me, "Josie, did you summon her full spirit?"

I nodded. He said, "Well, I am impressed. That is no easy task. How far are we from the village now? I suspect it will be in our eyeline soon."

Kimble told me, "Yes, it will be. He is right. The village is just over the mountain we are coming upon. We made it out of the valley, so this part should be easy. Once we reach the peak, you will be able to see the village."

Then, I told Malachi, "Kimble said we'd be able to see the village once we reach the peak of this mountain."

He nodded. "Let's go then!"

Excited to finally complete our task, the three of us smiled and laughed as Kimble ran us up the mountain's rocky slope. However, the higher we got, the steeper and more unstable the mountainside was. Kimble slowed down a lot. She and I were both tired, as we had taken the brunt of our second day's efforts. We reached the mountaintop in the early evening and we decided that we needed to use our third day after all. We found a small cave we could take refuge in, ate, and rested for the remainder of the night.

Malachi said to me as we sat by the fire that night, "Josie, I have to apologize to you. I put you at risk by overexerting myself like that. I do not know what I would have done if anything happened to you because of my reckless behavior. It was irresponsible of me. But I also need to thank you. It is thanks to your strength that we are here now. You are amazing, Josie. I owe you… my life. Still, next time, you need to keep the promise you made. It is too dangerous for you to worry about me."

I laughed. "You can worry about me, though? No, Malachi, that is not how this works. We are a team. We are friends. We worry about each other; we take care of each other. I will never, ever abandon you. You would never do that to me. Do not underestimate me, just like you are strong, I am strong too. Stronger than you or I realize and I will not sit by and pretend I am weak while my friend suffers. That is not the person you asked to join your team."

He smiled. "No, it is not. The person you are turning out to be, however, clearly is. You are spectacular, you know that? That passion, that purity, that strength. I love it. You remind me a lot of my mother in some ways."

I paused for a minute, then I asked him hesitantly, "Hey, Malachi, do you think of me as a sister?"

Malachi nodded. "Yes, how else would I think of you?"

I smiled and nodded. "Yes, I agree." Then, I thought how lucky I was to have a friend like Malachi. He is such a great guy. I hoped he and Johanna would work out. I thought they would be good together. So, I asked, "Malachi, do you have anyone back home you think of romantically?"

He laughed. "I do not think I have met the right woman yet. Why do you ask?"

I smiled a bit mischievously. "I was just wondering."

The following morning, we stood at the mountaintop and looked at the village from afar. We were finally going to make it back. We began the final stretch of our journey early and made it back to the village within a few hours. Upon our arrival, the Chief, Johanna, and most of the village were waiting for us at the gate. The Chief had tears in his eyes, "I am incredibly pleased. I see this young lady is quite amazing, not just anyone can summon a full-grown spirit fox to our world. And this young man is strong and has a noble heart. I never thought this day would come; the ones who will unite our islands have arrived. I would be honored, great heroes, if you would take Johanna with you on your journey as a representative of the undying support you have from the Island of Pallentine and its people."

Malachi and I smiled at each other, then he said to the Chief, "Of course, we will! Johanna will be a brilliant asset to our team and an even better friend. I look forward to working with Pallentine going forward."

The Chief replied, "Great Hero Malachi, when will you and your team be departing?"

Malachi answered, "I would like to set sail tomorrow morning. That should give Johanna time to prepare and us time to stock the ship up. We will be heading for the island of Nollent next."

Then, the Chief asked, "And if we need to get ahold of your team?"

Malachi explained, "You can send a message to Johanna anytime and as your representative, she will be the one to discuss it with the team."

The Chief agreed, then we all began our preparations. While we were preparing, I asked Malachi to tell me a bit about Nollent, this is what he told me:

"Nollent is torn in two. It will be the only island from which we need two representatives. Its northern half has access to much stronger runes than its southern half, and they use their resources and power to oppress the southern half. For any island to make peace with Nollent as a whole, Nollent must first make peace with itself. So, both north and South Nollent will have to send a representative, two good Nollentines that want peace, not just ones that are following orders."

"What kind of runes do they use?"

"Ground."

"And how is that different from Pallentine?"

Malachi laughed. "Pallentine uses nature language runes. They cannot move the ground; they can just communicate with the world around them.

When Johanna saved you before, she did not move the ground, she asked the ocean to save you. I thought I explained this to you before."

I nodded and thought back to that time when she said she asked "him" for help. "Yes, I just imagined it a bit differently. Does she command the ocean?"

"No, she has befriended it. The sky, the wind, and the trees too. She can communicate with many parts of nature, Josie, not just the ocean." He laughed at my confusion; this was all still so new to me. "To her people, they are friends. Most of the islands find it strange that they befriend nature, which is why her people are isolated culturally and socially, most places will not even trade with them out of fear that they will be cursed. I want to help them. As for the others that will join us, they must be good people. If we do not get along or they are not good people, the team does not work and the mission fails."

I nodded. "That is so cool; the power to befriend nature. We still all have different personalities. So who knows what they will be like. It should be interesting to meet all these different kinds of people throughout this journey."

Malachi agreed and told me not to worry. After we finished preparing, we all got some rest so we would be ready to set sail tomorrow. I was excited to be traveling with Malachi and Johanna. Johanna seemed excited too. In the middle of the night, she woke me up saying, "Josie… Josie!"

"Huh? Johanna? What is it?" I replied.

"I can't sleep, I'm too excited," she answered.

I sat up. "I am excited too. It will be fun, really."

"What type of people do you think we will meet next?"

"I asked Malachi the same thing. I am sure they will be great."

She agreed, then asked, "What is it like on Malachi's boat?"

"It is comfortable, honestly. Once you get used to it at least. It is kind of nice being able to look out at the ocean so freely and sit on the deck together. I usually do the cooking. We have some fun, for sure," I explained.

She smiled. "There is no way I can sleep now. Maybe we should leave early."

I agreed. "Let's go ask Malachi." But when we went to open the door, Malachi was already outside. He said to us, "Hey, ladies, I am sorry. I just could not sleep. I am anxious to get going."

I giggled. "Actually, we were coming to ask you if we could leave early because we are too."

He nodded. "I will go tell the Chief that we are going to set sail immediately." As he turned and left, Johanna and I jumped up and down, laughing and giggling in excitement. When Malachi returned, he told us the Chief had granted us permission to set sail immediately. We all gathered ourselves and headed to the ship quickly. The Chief met us there to say goodbye. As per the Pallentinians' custom, he gave each a prophecy prior to our departure.

To Malachi, he said, "Malachi, you are a strong young man with one of the best hearts I have seen in a long time. The legend of the great heroes lives inside of you. But to achieve your grand ambitions, you must face the darkness inside you so it does not have to consume you. The choice is yours. Blood does not define destiny. I see both and I must tell you, they are not the same."

Then, he turned to me and said, "Josella Marie Spade Lucietta III, that name will go down as a legend in and of itself. You are strong, ravishing, and pure of heart. However, you will meet those soon who you will long for deeper than anything else. That longing each of you will feel will either destroy you or save them. It is a thin line; I advise you to walk it carefully."

Finally, he spoke to Johanna. "My dearest Johanna, both love and friendship await you on your journey. However, I must warn you, if you wish to keep them both, you will need to remember that those who love you will not seek to hurt you, otherwise you may lose one, or both, and fail to be happy overall as a result."

Then he continued, "This is the wisdom I leave to the three of you. Please, take care of yourselves."

"You too, Chief," Malachi replied as he headed for the ship.

"Thank you! See you later!" replied Johanna as she waved goodbye.

Kimble stepped up beside me, then we began to walk towards the boat as I waved and said, "Bye!"

Finally, we loaded onto the ship and prepared to set sail. It was a five-day trip to Nollent. We had enough supplies to last us the entire trip, the Chief was very generous. Once we finished our preparations, Malachi began to steer the boat so we were on course. The three of us stood side-by-side looking up at the nightside. Malachi stood in the middle and took both mine and Johanna's hands, while Kimble lay by my left side. I contemplated our futures and the Chief's shared wisdom; I think we all did.

We stood there for about ten minutes in silence before Johanna finally said, "Well, here we are. What now?"

Malachi replied to her, "I guess we should celebrate our newest member joining us."

I nodded in agreement, then said, "I'll prepare some drinks and stuff." Before quickly heading to the kitchen, leaving Malachi and Johanna there.

While I was preparing things in the kitchen, Malachi and Johanna were talking. He asked her, "So, what is your story? Why do you want to join our mission anyway?"

She answered, "Umm, when I was young, members of Oceanica's Royal Navy murdered my mother and father because they refused to understand our ways and we refused to conform to theirs. I just want to live in a world where my people can be who they are and other people can be who they are and we do not have to hate each other because of it. I think we should embrace our differences. If that is too much to ask, I will settle for not having to defend my own differences."

Malachi smiled. "I do not think that is too much to ask at all. Our differences are what make us unique, living in a world where we all thought the same would be boring. You miss so many great people when you refuse to see past something as simple as them being from another culture. The truth is your people are cool. I like Pallentine. It is beautiful. And you have a good heart and a strong mind. I respect you and I am glad you are here."

Johanna nodded, then asked, "Hey, Malachi, do you think I'm attractive?"

He replied, "As a person or as a woman?"

"As a woman, I guess."

He paused. "Johanna, I do not think now's the time for me to think of anyone as a woman. We have a long journey ahead of us and there is so much going on in the world. I have to prioritize my mission; it would be unfair for me to see anyone as a woman right now."

"I can wait for an answer as long you need me to; you are the kind of man I'd consider worth waiting for," she replied.

He laughed, "Do not waste your time waiting for me, Johanna. I am no good for you."

"That's my decision to make, isn't it?"

"Yes, I suppose that it is."

I walked back onto the deck at that point and could feel the tension between the two of them. I was not sure what was happening, so I smiled as big as I could and said, "Okay! Who is ready to party? Shall I get some music going?"

I saw Malachi coming out of deep thought as he said, "Yes! Let us enjoy ourselves!"

Malachi and I began to eat, drink, and dance. But I noticed Johanna was still sitting there quietly. I went over to her and asked her, "Johanna, what is bothering you?"

She explained what had happened, then I asked her, "Does that not mean there is still hope? That he might look at you that way one day?"

She smiled. "Perhaps it does! Thanks, Josie! Anyway, now is not the time for this sobbing; it is a party. Let us have fun!"

After that, we all enjoyed ourselves and the rest of our night. Finally, we decided to rest. I figured I would clean up in the morning. So, Johanna, Malachi, and I all said good night and went to our cabins.

4

The following morning, I awoke to Johanna knocking on my cabin door, rushing me to get up. Kimble, who slept in my cabin, jumped up immediately. I, however, took a little longer. I yelled to Johanna, "What is going on? Why such a rush?"

"Just hurry!" she replied.

"I am coming, I am coming. Give me a minute."

I got up and quickly pulled myself together. After I finished, Kimble and I headed up to the deck. When I got up there, I said, "Okay, I am here. Now, what is going on?"

Malachi replied, "Look."

I looked up from rubbing my eyes and saw the most amazing thing. The sky had been painted different shades of orange and red as two dragons flew through it. One was black with large horns and the other was green with teeth like daggers. It was a breathtaking scene. The way I was taught, dragons were merely creatures from fairy tales told to children. I never imagined I would be standing right beneath one. I asked Malachi and Johanna, "Are we in danger? I mean, they could certainly kill us."

Johanna responded, "Probably not. Dragons usually do not bother with humans unless we do something to trigger them to do so. I do not believe any creature has a naturally violent temperament. Dragons are unusually proud creatures, so offending them will result in your death. That much I can say without doubt. We are no more fascinating to them than ants are to us. Would you go out of your way to destroy an ant or bother it if it were just walking by you on the road?"

"No," I replied. "Of course not."

After watching for a few more minutes, we got to work for that day. We each had our duties to attend to while traveling. Malachi would steer the ship as usual. Johanna would use her navigational skills to help map out the best course. I would clean and prepare meals for us. Kimble was just along for the ride unless we needed her, so she slept and relaxed for the most part. One thing is for sure, though; she ate a lot. It turns out, spirit animals eat more because they need more energy to maintain physical forms. If she did not, Malachi and Johanna would not be able to see her anymore, which I imagine would be lonely. I was glad to be her friend, and glad she had chosen me, but I wanted her to have other connections too. She deserved that much, so I did not mind cooking the extra food for her.

Halfway through that day, I finished everything I had to do until dinnertime. So, I decided to ask Malachi and Johanna if there was any way I could help them. I went to Malachi first, and he suggested that he teach me how to steer. He explained to me that it would take a few weeks to learn, but after I did, we could steer in shifts and it would give him a chance to rest. I felt him getting rest was important because he was the busiest of us, so naturally, I agreed to learn. It sounded fun anyway.

Malachi took his time explaining it all to me. There was a lot more to it than I had realized. I had to pay mind to the sails, the stars at night, the position of the sun during the day, the map, and the wheel. Plus, everything around us so we do not hit anything. As I was holding the wheel, Malachi noticed it was a bit off. So, he put his arm around me trying to show me where to hold the wheel again. He explained, "Look closely. The spoke at the top of the wheel is slightly longer than the others. If it is at the top, we are going straight."

I nodded to let him know I understood. However, Johanna walked in at that moment and said, "Josie, how could you?" Then she ran off.

Immediately realizing what she thought, Malachi took the wheel so I could run after her. She had barricaded herself in her cabin. I knocked and she yelled, "Go away! I do not want to see you right now, Josie."

"Johanna, you have to believe me. He was just teaching me how to steer. It was not like that. Please, believe me. I would not do that to you, I promise. You are my friend and that means the world to me, it really does."

"I will take your word for it. But Josie, are you sure Malachi does not see you in that way, even though it is not how you see him? He acts differently with you."

I laughed. "I think that is a good sign. Malachi treats me like his little sister, you do not want him to treat you like that; you want him to treat you like an equal. You have to be his equal if he is going to see you romantically."

She thought about it for a moment, then agreed, saying, "You have a point. Thank you, Josie. You really are a great friend. Let us go back to the deck."

I nodded, and we headed back to the deck where Johanna made her report to Malachi, then he and I continued our lessons. She watched us and smiled from afar. I thought what I said had really resonated with her because she seemed much better. Malachi did too. After a while, he told me he would be back and went to the kitchen to get her a drink. When he brought it to her, he said, "Hey, Johanna, it looks like you have been working hard. I brought you some lemonade."

"Oh, thank you," she replied.

He smiled. "It is no problem. I just wanted you to know I appreciate you. I should get back; we are about to have to veer right and she is still learning. Keep up the hard work." Then, he returned to the wheel. I said to him, "That was awfully nice of you."

"Yes, well, she deserved it." He looked away.

I chuckled. "You like her."

He got visibly nervous and said, "I like a lot of people. I am a friendly person. Plus, she is very likable."

I laughed hard. "You *really* like her."

Malachi just scoffed and kept working. A few minutes later, one of the dragons above us came falling from the sky into the ocean. Acting out of instinct, I dove into the water to help it Looking back, I do not know what I thought I was going to do. As I leaped from the boat, Malachi and Johanna screamed, "No!" but it was too late. I had already made up my mind. Kimble followed me and used her strength to get me and the dragon to the top of the water; since she could grow and shrink in size willingly, it was easy for her. The dragon woke only a moment after we got to the top of the water and said, "Who do you think you are, human? I am disgraced to be saved by you and this pathetic fox that serves you."

I responded, "Excuse me, Mr. Dragon, it is better to be disgraced than to be dead. I think I am the woman who just saved your life, so please, do not speak about my friend and me that way." Somehow, I managed to disregard the fact that this giant beast was towering over me as I confronted him.

The dragon scoffed, "My name is Hembron, the dragon of the eastern mountains. And as much as I hate to admit it, you are correct, human girl. I owe you my life and I do intend to repay my debt. But first, I must ask you for a favor."

"What is this favor?" I asked.

"Jentoli, my brethren from the western mountains, has decided to launch an attack on the humans. Regardless of my dislike for humans, I am aware that this is not the right thing to do. However, Jentoli is far stronger than I am. You are powerful, and from the looks of it, you travel with the true Prince of Tendu and a powerful young Pallentinian. Together, we may have the power to stop him."

I smiled. "Of course, we will help. It is no problem."

Hembron sneered. "You aren't going to ask your teammates what they think?"

I laughed a little. "I don't need to; I know who they are."

Hembron replied, "There is something unique about you three, that is for sure. Have your fox friend shrink me so I can come onto the ship."

I asked Kimble, "You can shrink other beings?"

She replied, "Only beings of magic or spirit beings. I need your help, though, since I've bonded myself to you."

"What is it I have to do?"

"Remember how you connected with my spirit before, I need you to connect with the dragon's so I can manipulate its size. It will not be as easy to connect with as mine was because it belongs to a physical magic being, but I should be able to give you some guidance."

I nodded and then Kimble said, "Okay, now close your eyes. Breathe slowly and deeply. Focus on the spirit plane, imagine it. Once you are there, tell me."

After a moment, I found myself surrounded by spirits. I had reached the spirit world. I said to Kimble, "I'm here."

"Okay, now call out to Hembron in your heart and in your soul. Let me know once you find him."

It took a few minutes, but I found him and I told Kimble. So, she continued, "Now, I need you to connect with him. Find a way to bond with his spirit. Then, I will have the freedom to use my power."

Having no clue how to bond with a dragon's spirit, I decided to try talking to it. After about thirty minutes, I had still gotten nowhere with the spirit. I asked it, "Do you not want to bond with me?"

He replied, "Of course, I do not. You are a human."

Finally, I asked Hembron, "What is so wrong with humans?"

He became angry, "You are weak, stupid, violent, useless, and destructive creatures that care nothing about anyone besides yourselves."

"You're right," I replied. "That's why things are the way we are. However, we are trying to fix it, my friends and I, that is. We are everything you claimed us to be, but I believe we can make things better. It is the wonderful thing about things being so bad, the only thing left to do is get better."

Hembron smiled. "You are a sweet girl, but you are awfully naïve. I want to believe in you."

I smiled back at him. "Well, who you choose to believe in is your choice."

Hembron nodded, then, I felt the bond form. Kimble suddenly appeared beside us saying, "You did it! My turn now." Moments later, we were back in the material world and Hembron was small enough to come onto the ship, so he flew over. Kimble carried me over and Malachi pulled us up. We explained the situation to him and Johanna quickly, they responded without a second thought, "Well, for what are we waiting? Let us go!"

Hembron guided us to the location of Jentoli's attack. When we arrived, it was a small village on the side of the remote mountain in the dragon's territory, it was not one of the islands of Rune. Kimble returned Hembron to his full size and then we waited for Jentoli to show. Malachi said to me, "Josie, you cannot really fight yet. You should wait for us somewhere safe. We will come to get you when the battle is finished."

I replied, "Malachi, shut up. I am not going anywhere."

Johanna, Hembron, and Kimble all laughed at my response. Malachi did too, after a moment. Then he said, "I know, I am overprotective. I guess I just have to trust your judgment." About an hour later, Jentoli showed. Hembron said to him, "Brother, I do not wish to harm you, but I cannot allow you to bring harm to the humans who live on the side of the mountain I have claimed as my home. I will not be dishonored in this way."

Jentoli responded viciously, "YOU harm ME? You are delusional, my dear brother. Stand down now, or you will die."

Hembron laughed. "Then I shall die with honor if I die at all."

Then, the fighting began. I hopped on Kimble's back and she began to fly up towards the dragons. I hadn't realized she could fly. I guess I had begun to realize there are many things she can do of which I am unaware. Malachi used flames from his feet to fly and Johanna asked the wind to lift her. Malachi and Johanna aided Hembron, but I sat there on Kimble's back frozen as I watched blood from the two dragons fall to the ground. My heart was breaking, there had to be another way. Finally, after what seemed like forever, I watched Jentoli fall to the ground and Hembron follow him down. All of us rushed down after them. Hembron said to Jentoli, "Brother, yield or I will kill you."

Jentoli replied, "Kill me, then, brother because if I live, I will attack again and again."

Hembron prepared to attack, but then, I called out without thinking, "Stop!"

Hembron paused and looked at me, still holding Jentoli down with his foot, and said, "What is it, girl?"

"He doesn't have to die," I said. "Brother killing brother, it is wrong. There is another way."

Hembron said, "By all means, share."

"I can purify his heart," I explained. "With Kimble's help, of course."

Hembron replied, "Do it, if you can."

Then Malachi interrupted, "No, Josie. Purifying a heart is dangerous. If you fail, his hatred will consume you and you spend eternity lost in the darkness in a part of the spirit world you do not want to go to."

I looked at him. "You will just have to trust me, Malachi, because I will not stand by and watch this senseless violence knowing there is another way. I have the blood of a priestess; this is what I am meant to do. Just as you are doing what you are meant to do, I must follow my path, understood?"

Malachi nodded. Then, Johanna wished me luck as I prepared to journey into Jentoli's spirit. Kimble would be coming with me. I had never purified anything before, so this was kind of a crazy idea. Kimble warned me, "Josie, I will not be of much help to you. I cannot function as a purification mechanism and protect you. You will have to hold your own in there."

I nodded hesitantly.

Then, Kimble and I went deep into the dragon's spirit. Everyone stood outside, watching, and waiting. To them, all three of us looked as though we were asleep, but they all knew much more was happening than what they saw. If Jentoli woke before me, I would not wake. If I woke first then I will have succeeded and Jentoli will be safe. That was all they could know, so they just waited. Each of them prayed. Hembron said to Malachi and Johanna, "Regardless of the outcome, please know, I am forever grateful to her. I would like to think of you all as friends if that is okay?"

Malachi replied, "Yes, please do. It is comforting to know that you see us that way."

Johanna agreed.

After that it was silent. Meanwhile, inside of Jentoli's spirit, Kimble and I were trying to purify, but the hatred in his heart was strong. I was struggling to protect myself from it while still purifying. Kimble was struggling too. I started to realize we were not likely to win this, so I told Kimble to leave and return to the material world. She refused, but I told her again, "Kimble, return to the material world. Leave me. If I get trapped, I do not want you to be stuck too. Be free, for me, please."

Again, Kimble refused to leave, "Josie, wherever you are, that is what I told you. If you are trapped, I am trapped with you. End of story."

I realized Kimble was not going to leave me, but, at that moment, I felt something. It was Johanna, her spirit was reaching out to me. She was praying. Then, I felt Malachi's and Hembron's too. I am a priestess! When people pray for me, it helps build my strength! I hoped that they would keep praying, that they would not give up on me. As they kept praying, the tides turned, it started to look like I could win. But I was exhausted, and so was Kimble. It still was not going to be easy. We needed to do it quickly, in one movement. So, Kimble and I stood back-to-back, it was as if we could read each other's minds, and moving perfectly coordinated we each went through the last step of the purification process as strongly as we could. Everything went black. I could not tell if we had won.

Hours later, I woke. Everyone was waiting at my bedside. Johanna asked, "Are you okay?"

I nodded.

Malachi said, "You did it, don't worry."

I smiled; then passed back out.

5

I woke up days later and went up to the deck. We were docked, but I could not tell where we were. I looked around and did not see anyone. But then, I saw Malachi and Johanna on the dock, and they ran over. Johanna said, "You're awake!"

I nodded, "Yes, where are we?"

"Nollent."

"Oh," I replied. "How long was I out for? Where is Kimble? What about Hembron and Jentoli?"

Malachi sighed. "Calm down, Josie. Everything is fine. You were only out for two days. Kimble is fine; she is just in my cabin because she did not want to bother you. As far as Hembron and Jentoli go, they are fine. They were incredibly grateful and they consider us friends. Hembron said Jentoli would be kept under close watch so we could be sure his heart was fully purified, but they seemed happy. As a token of their appreciation, they used a dragon's wish to get us here early. We have been sitting at the dock waiting for you to wake up so we could start looking for new teammates."

"You guys waited for me?" I asked.

Johanna laughed. "Of course, we did. The whole team needs to have input here."

We all smiled and I said, "Let's go, then!"

But Johanna said, "Wait up a second, Josie."

Malachi said, "Yes, you just got up. You need to eat something and make yourself look presentable."

It hit me that I was starving, and I nodded in agreement.

"Breakfast is on me this morning, okay?" Malachi said cheerfully. "We will go out. Get yourself together and tell Kimble to come on." I went and I did as he said.

We found a small café in town and decided to eat there. It was a cute little place and the server was sweet. I remember it clearly because it was while we were there that I saw him; he was on a stool across the café. I immediately felt drawn to this man, though I did not know why I had to speak to him. I excused myself and walked over to his table without thinking. I said, "Hello, I'm Josie." Unsure of where to go with the conversation, I stopped there.

He replied, "Hi, Josie, I am Kai. What can I do for you, beautiful?"

Kai was dark in tone. His voice deeper than the ocean, and it made me feel like I was melting. He had a bulkier build, but not too bulky, and the rune marks that riddled his arms and chest only made him more attractive. He was unbelievably handsome; I could not help but blush at his words. It was kind of bold that he flirted in such an obvious manner immediately; it somehow only led me to become more interested in him. I said to him, "I do not know, honestly. I just felt that I needed to know you. Do you believe in fate?"

He smiled. "I do today. Why don't you take a seat? I would love to get to know you some."

However, just as I sat down, Malachi came over. "Josie, we have to go."

I responded, "Malachi, we just got here. Do not be rude."

Then Kai asked, "Oh, is this your boyfriend?"

Malachi and I both said, "No!" at the same time. I explained that he was like my brother, Kai then said, "Oh, so you are just protective. Well, I am not going to hurt her. I like her quite a bit. She is mesmerizing. I have an unquenchable thirst for her already."

I could hear the sarcasm in his tone and I was not sure how to respond to being spoken about in such a manner, this man was extremely forward, so I struggled between pouting and smiling. Johanna interrupted my emotional crisis as she took Malachi's side saying, "Josie, you don't know this man."

I shrugged. "Well, I can get to know him, can't I?"

Johanna and Malachi were both upset by my response, Kai noticed it. He held my chin gently and moved his face closer to mine as he said, "Josie, my love, I do not want to cause any issues here. Your friends do not seem to like us talking very much. I am sure they will change their minds eventually, but for now, I should head out. Let us meet again soon, though, okay? Enjoy the rest of your day, baby girl." Then, he walked out of the café.

Angry, I turned to Malachi and Johanna. "What is wrong with you two? That was *very* rude. Especially you, Johanna! I am used to Malachi acting like I am a child, but I never expected that from you. You are supposed to be my best friend. I supported you and your feelings for Malachi even when you told me after speaking to him one time, and *this* is how you repay me."

Johanna replied, "Josie, I—"

But I interrupted her. "I do not want to hear it. There was nothing wrong with me speaking to that man. I am going after him. Please, if you care about me at all, do not follow me. If either of you does, I will never speak to you again." I ran after Kai. I could not explain it. Somehow, I just knew he was right. Malachi and Johanna stood in silence. I searched continuously for hours, yet I could not find Kai anywhere. I was upset.

It started to get dark out and it was beginning to rain. Just when I was going to give up my search, a group of strange men appeared in a circle around me. They started to try to grab me and pin me down. I screamed and tried to fight, but to no avail. I was ready to give up hope when suddenly, Kai came to my rescue. He quickly chased them off and ran over to me. My dress was torn and my corset was out. He was surprisingly respectful as he looked away. He even took off his shirt for me to wear. I looked up at his bare chest in awe, he was perfect. I tried to shake myself out of the trance that staring at him had put me in as I thanked him. I took his hand and he helped me to my feet. He replied, "It is no problem. I apologize that you had to endure such barbaric behavior. Come on, let us get you back to your friends. I am not leaving your side until I know you are safe again. Why were you off by yourself in the dark anyway?"

"I was looking for you," I replied.

He smiled. "You silly girl; your safety is far more valuable. I would have come to you eventually. Don't you know I feel the same thing? It is like gravity. We are being pulled together. For some reason, you are just someone who is meant to be in my life."

I smiled; he was such a gentleman. Malachi and Johanna came running up just as I went to reply to him. I guess they decided to come after me anyway. When they saw us, they assumed all the wrong things. Protective nature and jealousy had gotten the better of them. They got in stances as if they were going to attack Kai, but I interfered. "You idiots! He just saved my life!"

Johanna stopped dead in her tracks and bowed deeply. "I am so sorry. I may not like you much, especially not near Josie, but I appreciate your actions greatly. I hope you can see past my absurd behavior today. You see, Josie is special to me and I just wanted to protect her. I think of her as my best friend."

Malachi, however, still insisted on being rude. He muttered, "Sorry. Thanks." And said nothing more about the matter. I went to say something to him, but Kai stopped me. He said to them, "It is no problem, really. It was an honor. Josie is important to me too; I hope to find out in what way soon."

I asked Kai, "Will you join us, please? We are creating a team that will unite the islands and the mainland, end the injustices, and be a force for good."

Kai smiled. "If it is okay with your friends, I will. I do not exactly get the impression that they want me to join you."

Johanna sighed. "Just keep your hands off of Josie, okay?"

Malachi looked down. "I do not see what Josie sees, but I trust her more than anyone on the planet, no matter how naïve she may be. I will trust her judgment about you. However, take me seriously when I say that if you hurt her and destroy her purity, I will kill you and everyone you have ever known."

Kai chuckled. "I'd expect nothing less."

Excited, I said, "Great, now we only have to find one more representative from Nollent, the one from the north."

"I might know someone," Kai said.

I looked at Malachi and Johanna, then Malachi sighed and said, "Who?"

"My friend, Cal," explained Kai. "We have always been close, but the division between the north and south insists on making it difficult for us to be as close as we would like to be. You see, his family and mine are very much against it, so are most of the people around us. It also does not help that we are both men. I think if what you all are doing will help us be closer, he would be all for it. It is not fair that we must be separated because it makes other people unhappy. I mean, who cares? It is our relationship and we are happy."

I was shocked at what I was hearing. I thought he was interested in me, but it seems I was wrong. How could I have been so wrong? He is already with Cal; it is not possible. I tried to hide my embarrassment as Malachi nodded to him and said, "Bring us to him in the morning. For now, we should all get back to the ship so we can rest." Then he turned to me. "Josie, since bringing him was your decision, he is your responsibility. Show him to his cabin and make sure he is taken care of once we get to the ship." Then he turned back to Kai. "We will come back to gather your belongings tomorrow, okay?"

"Everything I own is with me, in the bag," Kai answered.

Malachi was even saddened by it, he said to us, "Josie, tomorrow take him into town to get him some more clothing and necessary products. You know where the spare coin is. And you, there are times where we need to present ourselves well, do not mistake this for charity."

Kai and I both nodded, then we all headed to the ship. I showed Kai to his cabin and made sure he had clean bedding and towels. I asked him, "Is there anything else you need?"

He smiled, "I need you to get some sleep for me, beautiful, you look tired."

I smiled back and asked him, "Kai, I was wondering about something. The way you talk to me, you do not talk like that to everyone, do you?"

He shook his head. "No, just to you and Cal."

I paused and just stood there quietly. He said, "Come sit down."

I sat at his bedside and he said, "Look, if I decide that I love you and Cal the same way, would it bother you?"

I giggled a bit at the thought of it. "I guess it depends on how I feel about Cal, doesn't it?"

He chuckled as I gazed at his perfect smile. His teeth were perfect. Is it weird that I even thought he had great teeth? Everything about him just mesmerized me. He finally regained his composure. "Well, then, we can discuss this once you meet Cal. For now, we can focus on just spending some time together. Let us just enjoy each other's company for the time being."

I nodded as he lifted me into the bed. I could feel his warmth as it radiated off his body. We talked for hours that night. He told me about his runes. They were particularly interesting to me. Apparently, two of his and Cal's were the same. They were the only two people that had ever been known to carry these runes. One was Wyrd, for fate, the other Jera, for celebration, endings, and beginnings. His third one was Algiz, which stood for self-interest or healing. It struck me as odd because he did not seem to be selfish at all. Cal's was Ehwaz for progress or adaptability. It felt good talking to Kai. I had never been able to connect with someone like this before, some part of me hoped that it would never end. Eventually, we fell asleep side-by-side. I realized it in the middle of the night and nearly had a heart attack fearing that I would be ruined. Who knows what the others would think of me now? Who knows what Kai would think of me? It was a tragedy.

6

The following day, Kimble and I woke up before everyone else so I could prepare breakfast, and so I could avoid being caught coming out of Kai's cabin. I did not want to have to explain myself. She kept me company while I cooked, eating anything I dropped while cooking. Once the meal was served, Malachi laid out a plan for the day.

"Josie, Kai, the two of you will go to town after this and get Kai some more appropriate clothing. After that, go meet up with your friend and bring him to the café we met at yesterday around noon. Johanna, I want you to come with me. The two of us will gather supplies and prepare for departure, if Kai's friend works out as our new teammate, we can leave Nollent tomorrow and head for Oceanica. I suspect they will be the hardest to find an ally in so I would like to get there as soon as possible. Plus, it is a two-week trip and we will likely have to stop for supplies in Mallishrine."

We all gave a nod and finished eating. Then prepared to head our separate ways for the day. Before Kai and I left, Johanna said to me, "Look Josie, I know you feel what you feel, but I can tell Malachi is really worried. To be honest, so am I. I am not saying you should not get to know him; I am just saying be careful, okay?"

I smiled. "If I say I'll be careful, will you talk to Malachi for me?"

She looked over at Malachi, then back at me. "I'm not sure how much good it'll do, but for you, I'll give it a try."

I laughed, then we all headed out. Kai and I found a few stores to shop in. It was fun. He was so confused. He did not even know his measurements, so we had to have them taken. He and I had great conversations throughout our time together, so I asked him, "Kai, are you genuinely interested in me? Or is this just for fun?"

Kai chuckled. "Sweet girl, mindless flirting is a habit I let go of some years ago. I am interested in you."

"Why is that?"

"Well, there is the obvious, you are gorgeous. But it goes beyond the superficial for me. You are a strong woman, fearless. You stand up for yourself and for those around you. You are pure of heart. You have this brilliance about you, it makes you stick out. It makes me want to protect you. I feel drawn to you, as if I could talk to you about anything, for hours. You make me have faith and I do not know why," he explained, then asked, "Why are you interested in me?"

"You are by far the most attractive man I have ever met. Besides that, you are kindhearted and understanding. You are also patient, which I need. Also particularly important, you seem as though you can deal with my stubborn nature well. Plus, I am drawn to you as well. Something about you makes me feel like you will be one of the most important people in my life."

Then, we continued about our day. I did not know what to expect as I continued down this path with Kai, but as I anticipated the possibilities, only amazing things came to my mind. Eventually, we finished our shopping and I said to him, "Let's drop this stuff off on the boat and head to your friend's.

He nodded in agreement, so we did. As we approached Northern Nollent, Kai warned me, "Stay nearby, please. Some Northerners do not take well to Southerners being on this side of the island and you clearly are not from here, so that will not help."

I nodded and we continued through the streets. We got many stares. One man even spat at us. Eventually, we arrived at the meeting spot. We were early, so we had to wait a while for Kai's friend. While we waited, I started asking questions about him. He had a more playful tone to his personality from what Kai said. I was looking forward to meeting him. He seemed interesting. When he arrived, he immediately dropped all his things to hug Kai. The first thing he said is, "I got your message. I understand the gist of the plan, I will meet these people and join up with the cause." Then, he turned to me, "You must be Josie. You are gorgeous. Do you want to kiss me?" He was very forward. He was also extremely handsome, but in a more unique way than Kai was. He had fair skin and a slender build, with blond hair and the bluest eyes I had ever seen. He looked like a prince character from a children's story. His playful tone was kind of sarcastic. It made him standoffish, as if he were protecting himself from something. I wondered what it could be that made him feel so vulnerable.

I did not know what to say, so I just stared at him. Kai intervened. "Cal, be nice to her, please."

Cal laughed. "I am, I am."

Then, we began to head back to South Nollent to meet the others. On the way, we all laughed and talked freely. I liked Cal, a lot. When we got to the café it turned out that the others did too, though they both mentioned that his playful flirting with me irritated them. It was all in good fun. Malachi and Johanna had finished the preparations for our departure, so the group decided to head back to the ship to throw a welcome party for Kai and Cal. While I was in the boat's kitchen preparing snacks and drinks, I overheard Kai and Cal in the hall.

Kai slammed Cal against the wall. *BANG!* "Cal!" he said passionately. "I missed you!" He hugged his friend tightly and then continued. "We're safe now. We don't have to hide it from her."

Cal replied, "Yes, we do. No one could ever understand what we did back then. She seems great, but we have to keep the wall up."

However, I had opened the door and was now standing in the hall with them. I cleared my throat to get their attention, when Cal saw me, he said to Kai, "Whatever, you tell her. But if she betrays us, it is your fault. Do not say I did not try to protect you from it."

As Cal walked away, I asked Kai, "Did I do something that made him distrust me? I would never betray the two of you."

Kai laughed. "You don't even know what we did yet?"

I shook my head. "It doesn't matter. You are both good people; I can tell."

Kai smiled. "You are so sweet, but sometimes I do not feel like a good person. It was almost two years ago now; Cal and I had just found each other. Our families, as I told you, did not take it well that we wanted to be close. Cal's father lost his temper in a drunken rage when he saw us together. Cal's blood was everywhere. Eventually, I realized that he was not going to stop. He would kill Cal if I did not do something. So, I tackled him. When I did, he fell and hit his head on the edge of a stone tabletop, he died. Normally, there would be nothing wrong with what I did, except I am from the South and he is from the North, even with Cal on my side, I would be killed for what I had done. So, Cal helped me to cover up his father's death. You are the first person we have ever told. It is not that Cal distrusts you. It is that he has a distrusting nature overall. For a long time now, we have only really had each other. What he just did could be considered being vulnerable, at least in Cal's book. I think if he continues to spend time with you, he will heal. I think we both will."

I smiled. It made me happy to hear Kai and Cal wanted to spend time with me, so I told him, "Thank you for sharing that story with me. I will not tell anyone, I think one day you will decide to tell the others too. You did the right thing, both of you did, with his father. I would never hold something you did to survive against you, Kai. I will make sure Cal knows that too. I will take care of you both, the best I can. You have my word, okay?"

Kai laughed. "That makes me really happy, Josie. But if you are not careful, we will both fall in love with you."

I smiled, but I could tell he was only half joking. Thinking about it, I realized I would be lucky to have him or Cal. They were both great men. The thought lingered in my mind for the rest of the day and into the night, as the party went on. Cal had so many barriers, but something inside of me drove me to want to get through them and be close to his heart. Meanwhile, Kai was an open book that laid his heart at my feet almost immediately, and I felt like

I wanted to care for him because of that. They were both so special. I still managed to have fun at the party even with these thoughts lingering in my mind. I got to know Cal a lot more. At one point, when he and I were isolated behind a little bit, he said to me, "Thank you, Josie." Then dragged me into the middle of the ship to dance. Only a moment later, Kai joined us too. However, I soon noticed that Malachi and Johanna had been caught up in some intense conversation for a while now. They seemed happy. I wondered what happened with them that day, but I would not find out until the following day.

Soon, it had gotten late and we all went to bed. I petted Kimble's head as I lay in my cabin when I heard a light knock on the door. It was Cal, "Josie, can I come in for a moment?"

"Yes, come in."

He opened the door and sat at my bedside when he asked me, "Do you think I'm a good person, Josie?"

I nodded. "Of course I do, Cal."

Cal smiled. "Then, I guess as long as you and Kai think so, that is all that matters to me. People may have opinions about me because of the rumors that I killed my father, but if you and Kai say I am good, I must be. You two are the best people I know. Thanks." Then, he hugged me tightly, however, he slowed down as he began to let go. His lips moved closer to my ear and he whispered, "You're going to be mine."

Then, Kai burst in and said, "Cal, stop harassing Josie and come on, it's time for bed."

Cal got up and wrapped his arm around Kai, the two of them left my room laughing mischievously. I had not the faintest clue what was going on. I decided that it was time Johanna and I gave each other some updates. I was sure she felt the same way. So, tomorrow she and I would talk after we set sail for Oceanica. However, as it turns out, we would not be setting sail the following day as we had planned.

I woke to the smell of flames and screaming, by the time I ran to the deck the others had managed to put out the fire. But the damage to the sails and other parts of the ship was bad. "Why would someone do this?" I asked.

Kai looked down. "It isn't uncommon for angry Southerners to burn or vandalize the property of foreigners because they feel that they don't belong here."

Cal sighed. "This will put our timeline back quite a bit. Repairs will take a while, and they will not come cheap."

Malachi shook his head. "Okay, we knew this would not be easy. Everyone pick your heads up and get to work. Kai, Cal, you are natives. You can get materials cheaper than we can. Can you go buy them for us? I will send you a list. Johanna, Josie, and Kimble, you all stay here and start cleaning this mess up. Johanna, you look out for Josie, please. I will go inventory supplies to see what was taken or damaged, then I'll make Kai and Cal's list. After that, I will see if I can find out who did this. If we can help the culprit, rather than punishing him, we may be able to gain some support locally and it will do us good after the team is fully assembled. Got it?"

We all nodded and got to work. It was not long before the boys had left the ship, it only took Malachi an hour to inventory our supplies and put together a list for Kai and Cal. After that, it was just Johanna, Kimble, and me. Kimble had found a cat aboard the ship as we cleaned that she made friends with. I found it odd being that it was just an ordinary cat, not a spirit animal. It was cute to see them together, though. This was okay; it gave Johanna and me a good chance to talk. I asked her, "Did something happen between you and Malachi yesterday? You seem… closer."

She smiled. "Not really, but yes still."

"Explain?" I replied, my curiosity was piqued.

"Well," she began, "he was pretty upset about Kai yesterday. As we walked, he was muttering all kinds of things. So, I mentioned to him that I wanted to protect you too. However, the fact that you are naïve in nature did not make you any less of a woman, that you were amazing and that men were going to be attracted to you. Naturally, he mentioned that many men would be attracted to you for the wrong reasons. He thought that they may seek to take advantage of your spiritual prowess or your latent beauty. But I told him that acting as we did would push you away and the best way to protect you from men like that was to let them into our circle where we could watch them. That way, if they did anything to hurt you, we could be there for you. He saw reason eventually and thanked me for my counsel. He said any successful or intelligent man seeks counsel in the wisdom of the women around him, especially those close to his heart. I realized then; he was telling me I was close to his heart. I assured him that I would always be there for him and I would support him in any way I could. After that, I just got the sense that he wanted to be around me more and that he really trusted me."

I smiled and said, "Keep that up and he won't be able to resist you."

She laughed. "What I said to him was true. Even if he never returns my feelings, he is a good man and I believe in what he can do for this world wholeheartedly. I will always stand by his side; in whatever way, he decides to let me stand there."

I looked up at the sky and said, "You know, that is probably why he will fall in love with you. It is selfless love, which is something hard for a man like Malachi to find."

Johanna nodded and looked as though her mind began to linger, then asked, "What about you, Kai, and Cal? What is that dynamic I am seeing?"

I shook my head. "I do not know, honestly. I get the sense they both care for me in a romantic way, though it is hard for me to tell how serious Cal is. But then, I also get the sense they care for each other in the same way and have not admitted it. The situation is hard to read."

Johanna was shocked, "How? They are both men—"

"What does that matter?" I asked.

"I guess it does not. Gender is such a silly thing to think about when a force as powerful and great as love is in question, don't you think?" she said.

I nodded in agreement. "It is. I still wonder, though, how do they feel about me? And how do I fit into their feelings for each other?" I had to ask her. Some part of me still felt unsure. I mean, even if Kai already made his feelings clear, it still did not feel as if I had clarity. It felt as if it were just a joke or was unrealistic for them to feel that way about me, perhaps it has to do with how I was raised that I would think such a relationship is impossible.

Johanna laughed a bit after her brief pause. "Maybe you can be with both. Think about it, they will be together and neither of them will have to give you up. If you all fall in love with each other, what is the issue?"

I paused, then said, "I do not know if I can be in a relationship like that, though. It is not how I imagined my life. I was taught to be a proper lady growing up, to marry at or above my station and to always conduct myself in a manner that proper society finds acceptable."

Johanna looked at me. "You do not know for sure that is the situation. They might know the situation for sure. But Josie, do not hold out for what you imagined because what you find might be better, even if it is not tradiional. And what you imagined might not be all you thought, even if tradition told you it will be. You do not have to be who you were raised to be; I think you just being who you truly are is the best version of you."

Johanna's words made sense to me. I contemplated them as I continued cleaning. The fire really made a mess around here. We finished just as Malachi returned. "I found the culprit," he said as he dragged the man aboard the ship.

"Look, I am sorry. You do not understand what it is like. Please do not kill me," the man pleaded.

We all began to laugh uncontrollably when Johanna said, "Sir, we are not going to kill you. That is ridiculous!"

Malachi added, "We saw what you did to our ship and while it was wrong and caused us a lot of trouble, we realize that you must be angry about something."

Then I jumped in, "So, we wanted to see if there was anything we could do to help you or your family."

We all laughed a little more as the man relaxed. Kai and Cal returned to the ship as the man began to explain, "My daughter, she is only eight years old and was kidnapped by foreigners and dragged onto a ship. I thought it was this one, but I was wrong. But I still had to pay the men I hired to help me, so we stole your stuff and set a fire. I do apologize, but please, help me find my daughter if you can."

At that moment, we all got serious. I said, "Of course, we will do everything we can."

Johanna immediately began talking to every plant and animal around to see what they knew. Kimble and I flew around and searched from the sky for anything suspicious. Malachi asked around at the docks. Kai went to some old friends to see if any rumors were circulating with the locals. Cal went with the old man to the abduction site to look for clues and see if the person left a trail for us to follow.

We met back up at the boat a few hours later and everyone shared what information they had found. Kai had heard rumors of a child trafficking ring that recently surfaced, Malachi heard about a story the children had been telling about a boat on the docks and how if you get on it, you will never return. I saw a strange-looking boat with no name on the side of it and the men on the ship looked anxious as if they were hiding something. Now that we knew that boat was our target, we decided we would attack tonight and free all the children aboard.

When the time came, we launched our attack. Sneaking around was not really our style, so we kind of went all out. Malachi's flames were shooting everywhere, while Johanna had decided to go old-school and fight them hand-to-hand, the ground power of Kai and Cal's runes were amazing too. They moved totally coordinated, even when they fought together. You could tell how close they were. And while they caused a commotion, I snuck down to the lower deck with Kimble to save the children. There were a few guards posted at the door, so Kimble attacked them to get them out of my way. I quickly freed the children, then got them to safety as quickly as possible.

By that time, the others had finished fighting and had tied up the men for the police to come to retrieve them. We found a list documenting all the children that were sold and to whom as well, so we turned that over too, so they could be rescued. We did not have the manpower to save them all ourselves. Malachi assured me that we would check in on the investigation to be sure that it was being managed properly, though.

That night, I made a feast to celebrate our victory. Many of the locals, including the man who attacked our ship, came to thank us for what we did. We made friends with them and eventually, the time came for the celebration to wind down. It had been another long day; I was getting used to those. I thought back on our journey thus far and looked around at all the friends I had made, it made me realize how far I had come from that spoiled brat who threw a fit to get away from her guard and called Malachi a peasant. I was incredibly happy here, with these people, they were my home now. We all decided to get some rest, as we would begin our repairs the following day.

I said good night to everyone, then Malachi came over and said, "Josie, wait!" When I stopped and turned around, he continued, "I wanted to apologize to you. I mean, I am going to apologize to Kai and Cal as well, but to you too. The way I have been acting is not cool. They seem nice and I am glad they are here. You made a good call. I still wish you would not think of anyone romantically, but that is your choice to make and I am sure whoever you end up with will be amazing."

I smiled and said, "Thank you, Malachi. Good night now."

"Night, Josie," he said as we each headed to our cabins.

7

The three days we spend repairing the ship were rather interesting ones. The thing about team and friendship is that sometimes being close to other people comes with challenges in and of itself. Spending too much time with those you love, especially in an isolated space, like a boat, can cause many arguments to arise. Malachi told me early the first day that my job throughout this process would be to make sure food and drinks were available throughout the process to keep the crew energized and maximize the work we got done. He also asked me to clean up behind the repair work when I found the time but made it clear that food and drink took priority. So, I took my orders seriously.

I made a hefty spread for breakfast with lots of options for everyone. Malachi enjoyed the bacon and sausage, with some pancakes. Kai and Cal ate nearly all the fresh fruit I had chopped. Johanna had some eggs and toast. Kimble ate a little of everything. By the time they had all finished, there were only scraps of food left, so I did not eat. I did not mind, though, not at first anyway. I just cleaned up the mess they had left and went back to the kitchen to prepare snacks and some fresh lemonade to set out. When I finished, I set them out on the deck's table, then saw an enormous pile of trash off to the side. I walked over and began to clean it, but as I lifted the heavy bags, Johanna walked over with another and said, "Oh, you are taking the trash. Can you take this one too?" And without even waiting for my reply, she tossed the bag into my arms and walked away.

I struggled to carry the bags of trash off the ship and as I came onto the dock, I fell, spilling trash everywhere. Of course, I had to clean it up before it fell into the ocean. I looked up onto the ship to see if anyone could help, but no one was in sight. So, I sighed and cleaned the trash up on my own, then lugged each bag into the disposal bin one by one. When I returned to the ship, I was out of breath, but Kai and Cal immediately ran over to me and Cal said, "We're out of snacks." As he finished eating the last of the ones I had made.

Kai added, "Lemonade too, can you make some more?" Then they both walked off without ever paying mind to the fact that I was covered in trash. I began to get frustrated, but I decided not to react. I took a deep breath, went to the kitchen, and prepared lunch, more snacks, and plenty of lemonade. I took it out to the deck and once I set up the table, I went to make my plate. Malachi said to me, "Whoa! Do not be greedy, Josie. Let the crew eat first. They have been working hard."

Kimble added, "Yes, Josie, you can wait a minute. They are nice enough to do all the challenging work, the least you can do is let them eat first."

At that moment, I felt as though I was going to burst, but again, I did not. I chose to remain calm and I said, "You all are right, that was rude of me. Go ahead, everyone." Then, I stepped aside. After, there was no food left, again. I stood in the kitchen muttering to myself, "How dare they? They do all the challenging work. Because what I am doing is so easy, right? How clueless can they be? And they just keep piling on. Someone needs to put those simpletons in line, they act like they were raised by animals. No, animals are more civilized than that," I muttered on and on as I continued to cook.

These incidents continued to happen all day until finally, I snapped. I hollered at all of them, "How dare you fools? I have been slaving away all day and not once have any of you thanked me, absolutely no appreciation. And do you want to know what is worse? I have not eaten because you have not left me ANY food, but all I have done is cook. And I reek of trash because of that extra bag Johanna assumed I could carry when I already had three in my hands earlier. Yet, I was called rude for trying to eat prior to you idiots! Yes, of course! Now you all stare at me as if I am insane because I have lost my temper. Well, I have news for you, my ability to conduct myself as a lady only goes so far. Even I draw the line somewhere. Now, I am retiring to my cabin to bathe. The smell of this trash is making me nauseous. Keep the stupid food." Then I stomped off. They all stared at me silently.

I sat in the tub crying out of irritation, then, I let out a screech. After a while, I pulled myself together enough to get out. I put on a night gown and got comfortable. Then, my stomach grumbled. I was hungry, but I did not want to leave my cabin and risk running into anyone on the way to the kitchen. I was still a bit angry, but I was also kind of embarrassed that I had gone off the way I did. It is not often I behave in such a deplorable manner, after all. So, I just sat there. However, Kai came and knocked on the door after a few minutes. He said to me, "Josie, we are sorry. We were idiots."

Then, I heard Cal, "Josie, you know we would never take you for granted on purpose, right? We love you, all of us. We know how much you do. This team could not make it without you. Please, you must believe us. I think we all just got a little too comfortable and used to having you there. Sometimes, it is hard to imagine you not taking care of all of us. But today, we should have taken care of you better. If you come out, I promise, none of us will ever make that mistake again, especially not me and Kai, we honestly cannot afford to lose you, Josie."

I sighed and opened the door, "I love you guys too, come on, let's go see Malachi before he falls apart." I hated fighting with them, I just wanted to leave it be. It is never a good feeling when there's conflict with loved ones, but it is nice to know that no matter how much we fight and argue, we will always work it out and be there for each other at the end of the day.

Kai laughed. "It may be too late for that. Malachi fell apart the moment he realized you were angry; you know how he is when it comes to you." It made me laugh a bit. I guess Malachi was a bit strange when it came to me. He was this odd combination of overprotective, melodramatic, and overly affectionate. That is why I always saw him as a brother, though. When I got to the deck, I found a nice meal on the table, Malachi said, "It is all yours. Eat, relax, and call us if you need anything."

Then Johanna said, "And don't worry about cleanup, we got it."

I smiled and said, "Thanks, guys. It means a lot to me that you would do this." After that, I enjoyed the rest of my peaceful night. Of course, the following day had a whole new set of dramatic issues. Johanna and Malachi got into some sort of argument; I was unable to deduce the cause. However, it somehow led to them fighting. They had decided the winner would be the team's leader. There was not much I could do to stop them, so I decided it best to let it play out. Though, I already knew who would win the fight.

Kai, Cal, Kimble, and I all lined up on the edge of the ship to watch as they prepared to fight. Tension built up and finally, Johanna asked, "Are you ready?"

"Hold on," Malachi replied; then he released his runes and said, "Now I'm ready."

Johanna launched the first attack but missed Malachi. She was the only one launching attacks but she could not hit him. She demanded that he explain himself, so he did. "I do not have to attack you to win this fight, Johanna. You will forfeit it; I just need to evade your attacks until you do."

"Forfeit?" she exclaimed. "You must have the wrong woman; I am a warrior."

"But you are a woman nonetheless, are you not? A woman who has decided something of great importance," he replied.

She contemplated his words as she continued to launch attacks, then realized, she was a woman that decided to stand by Malachi no matter what. She paused at that moment and said, "I decided to stand by you. I apologize, Malachi. I may not agree with you, but I will support you."

Malachi smiled, "And I may not agree with you, Johanna. But please trust that I will take your thoughts on the matter into consideration regardless of them being different from my own. I value your opinions greatly and I would never blatantly ignore you when making such a decision. I will take precautions, even though I do not think what you said will happen."

Johanna smiled sweetly and Malachi brushed her hair back out of her face. Then, he laughed a little. "I don't know what I'd have done if one of those attacks had landed, I'm strong, but physically, you far outdo me."

She nodded. "I'm no match for your level of magic, though I could never get to your body without being burned to a crisp, at least not if you were serious about the fight." It seemed that the matter had been settled, Kai and Cal looked confused. I snickered and told them, "You'll get used to it." When I thought about it, Johanna and Malachi made perfect sense for one another. They had the utmost respect for each other and they were both immensely powerful, though it was true that Malachi was far more powerful. They were both loving, committed, and intelligent people with good hearts and strong minds. They worked because they understood one another perfectly, even when they disagreed. They could communicate in a way that was different. It was like they lived on a separate plane from the rest of us.

Kimble laughed a little when I did. It turns out our ship had taken some of Johanna's attacks, so we would not be able to finish repairs that day, we would need just one more. Her destructive power was marvelous. It certainly caught my eye at least. We worked hard for the remainder of the day, then rested well, and when the third day began, we were determined to get done. Everyone put their best efforts forward, but there was still so much to do and we were all exhausted. It was the longest day of all, but come nightfall, the repairs were finished. We planned to sail the following morning.

Kai and Cal helped Malachi. Johanna mapped the best course, including us stopping for more supplies about a week into our travels. And Kimble and I went into town to buy some last-minute grocery items I needed. I will not lie; it was nice to get some space from the rest of the team. Tomorrow, we would be off to Oceanica to finish building our team. Then, we could start to heal this world. It was all great but spending so much time together could be stressful.

I began to wonder if the tensions were because we were so close to one another. Do you know how sometimes the people closest to you can irritate you in a special way? It felt a lot like that. I just thought maybe if we all got some space that we would start getting along again. After a few hours alone in town, I did begin to wonder how the others were doing. I kind of missed Kai and Cal. Things were always so exciting and unpredictable when they were around. I did not make it back to the boat until late, so I went straight to bed. From what I could tell, everyone else did the same.

I began to fall asleep hoping that tomorrow we could all be together again. But just as I did, there was a knock on my door. I called out, "Who is it?"

"Cal. Kai is with me," he said.

"Come in," I said, and so they did.

"Hey, Josie, we just missed you today. Can we sit in here for a little while?" Cai asked.

Kai laughed shyly. "Cal, man, do not be so blunt. She is a lady."

I smiled. "No, it is okay. Have a seat, I missed you two, as well. It feels like we have not been able to just sit down and talk to one another in forever."

I genuinely had missed them. It brought me joy to see them smile as they sat down at my bedside. We did not end up talking much, but they did fall asleep sitting in those chairs with their heads resting on my bed. When I woke, I realized what happened. This is the second time a mistake like this has been made. However, I was not worried about my reputation this time. I was simply happy to see them looking so relaxed and peaceful. I looked over at them and had the overwhelming temptation to run my fingers through their hair, but I did not.

Instead, I just slipped out of the bed and tried to find Johanna. This urge to play in the hair of both boys, what did it mean? Did it mean what I thought it meant? I began to think it did. Johanna and Malachi were already preparing to set sail, though, so I could not disturb them. I did not know what to do. I had come to an overwhelming realization and I could not figure out how to manage it. The truth was, I had feelings for both Kai and Cal and I was fairly sure they both had feelings for me.

8

After pacing for a few minutes, I realized that no matter what I did, this was not a situation that would be resolved right now. The best thing I could do was go about my business for the day and just be conscious of what happens going forward. So, I went to the kitchen and started to prepare breakfast. I called for everyone to come to eat when I was done, By that point, we had already set sail thanks to the others. Everyone came rushing to the table and sat down. They all thanked me, then we all started to eat. It was the start of a good day.

We had a long trip ahead of us, so we had to be creative as we produced things to do in between our duties. Johanna and I talked a ton that first day. I got an update on things between her and Malachi. She told me as we were watching the stars that night, "Malachi called me 'baby girl' the other day. Should I take that platonically, or not?"

I laughed. "I don't think so."

"You don't think what, exactly?" she asked.

"That you should take it platonically."

Johanna got frustrated. "Josie, could you be any clearer about what you're saying?"

I laughed some. "Calm down, Johanna. I do not think that you should take it platonically. Malachi likes you, a lot. I can tell."

"Why won't he just say that, then? I hate when people do not just say what they mean," she said.

"Well, 'baby girl,' not everyone is blunt as you are. Malachi communicates through his actions more so than words," I told her.

She sighed. "I just want to hear him say it once. Kai and Cal tell you all the time, don't they?"

I giggled. "Actually, Cal has never told me he has feelings for me. I can just tell because it is Cal and I know him. Kai has said it in so many words, but never so plainly as you. I have not told either of them either. Some things do not have to be said when you have a bond with someone. And other times, you do need to hear the words, and it is okay for you to need that. But you must be willing to respect the other person enough to wait until they are ready to say them. If they love you, they will give you what you need, even if it takes them some time."

Johanna was surprised for a moment, then, she smiled as said, "Josie, sometimes you speak with the wisdom of the Chief himself. I have to wonder how someone so young came across such wisdom."

I laughed. "Somethings you just know." Then I looked down. "Other things, I guess you just don't."

Johanna asked, "Oh no, what's that about?"

I shook my head. "I care for them both. I don't want to choose, and I don't want to hurt either of them."

She put her arm around me. "Oh, beautiful, I do not think they would make you choose. I also do not think they would be hurt if you decided to be with them both. They will love you more for it, in fact. They always will. Their whole goal was to make things so they could be together. It is only natural they would love a woman that also allowed them to do so. If you think about it, the fact that you love them both may just make you perfect for them. Though, it may take them some time to realize that."

Johanna's words resonated with me as I went to bed that night. The second day was rather busy due to weather complications, so none of us had much downtime. It passed by quickly because of that, but it did not leave any room for us to enjoy ourselves. Luckily, the storm had passed by nightfall, so it did not prevent us from resting up for the following day.

On the third day, I spent my free time with Malachi. It was nice to hangout just him and me. We hardly ever got to bond one-on-one anymore. I realized that I had missed him even though we had been together the whole time. Likely because there was a time where it was just him and me. We just used to have more time to relax together and talk. He decided that he wanted to play some cards with me. While we played, we talked. I told him, "You know, Malachi, you should really learn to express yourself better."

He raised his eyebrow and asked, "Why do you say that?"

Then, I explained, "Sometimes, when you are not clear about your feelings, the people you care about get hurt. If you are not ready to say certain words, that is fine. But you should find a way to let them know still."

I assumed he would figure out what I was talking about, but he did not. His next words were, "Huh?"

I just laughed and said think about it. Then he said, "I actually had some advice for you as well. Stop being scared. If you want something, you should just ask. You will not know the answer until you do."

I paused, then asked, "What do you know?"

Malachi just laughed and then continued playing with his hand. A few minutes later, it seemed what I said clicked to him. He asked, "Wait, did Johanna mention something to you? What did I do?"

I laughed, then said, "I think it's more about what you didn't do."

He said, "I really screwed up. I have to go." Then ran off. I had no clue what he was doing, but I got the impression that he understood what I was saying. I stayed there and contemplated what he had told me. I looked at Kimble who was laying at my feet and said, "Just ask, huh?"

Kimble nodded, "Yes, of course, you should ask for something if you want it. It only makes sense. You know, Josie, I am sure that you are smarter than this. It is irritating to see you behaving in such a way. It is beneath you. Why don't we do some spirit training to keep you busy since you are wasting time asking stupid questions?"

I giggled some, then agreed. Kimble could be so strict as an instructor, but I loved knowing how much she cared about me. She took me into the middle of the deck and we meditated for a while. We practiced spirit attacks after and we did some spirit manipulation too. It turned out that both needed work. I guess it made sense because I had not much experience with either. Kimble told me, "Do not worry, Josie. You will get better. It takes a lot of practice to master spiritual prowess, trust me."

I nodded. We practiced a few more hours before I went to go prepare dinner. When I served the meal, we all sat down. While we ate, we engaged in some light conversation. Malachi mentioned at one point in the meal that he had something he wanted to give Johanna.

"What is it?" she asked him.

He took out a piece of parchment and handed it to her. After she read it, she seemed happier than ever. She told me later that it read:

"Johanna,

There is much that I cannot yet explain to you. I also cannot commit myself to you yet. Unfortunately, I also cannot say the words you wish to hear, though, I wish I could. If you are the woman that I believe you are, then I am sure you will understand that there will come a time that we will be right, but that it must be at a time when I can guarantee that it will not create more chaos in the world around us. Your Chief's warning is one I must heed. For now, it is my hope that you will accept these written words as a suitable compromise.

I love you…."

I was glad he took my advice and did something; it was nice to see them working things out in a way that worked for them. We all went to bed soon after that. When I walked into my cabin, Cal and Kai followed me.

Cal said, "Josie, we like sleeping in here. Can we keep doing that?"

I smiled and thought about what Malachi had told me earlier. They just asked, just like Malachi had said. Maybe he did have a point. So, I said to them, "Yes, you two can sleep in here from now on? But can I ask you two for something as well?"

Kai smiled. "Anything for you, my love?"

Cal nodded in agreement.

I laughed a little. "Can I play in your guys' hair?"

Cal smiled hard. "I would love that! What about you, Kai?"

Kai nodded. "That sounds wonderful, please do."

So, I lay down and they sat at my bedside again. When they laid their head on the edge of the bed, I reached my hand over and began to play in their hair. Cal's was thick and long. I enjoyed twisting and playing with it. Kai's hair was thinner and softer, my fingers ran right through it. I loved both, they seemed to enjoy it as well. They appeared happy and relaxed. After a bit, we had all fallen asleep. It was the best I had slept in a long time. I felt at peace having them by my side. I started to wish we had a bed big enough for us to all lay in, having them by my side would mean more than I could explain. Maybe one day we would.

The next few days came and went quickly. After the first week, we were running short on supplies. It was day seven and it was time to dock in Mallishrine to resupply. Mallishrine was a unique island full of people who had achieved spiritual enlightenment. It was the only island not involved in the constant inter-island conflicts and wars. Malachi said we did not need a representative from there because they would support just about anything that led to peace, so we would just be getting supplies. Based on Johanna's maps, it seemed Mallishrine was not far off at all, but I did not see it anywhere. So, I asked her, "Where is the island exactly?"

She explained, "Oh, it is just up ahead. Mallishrine is protected by a spiritual barrier so you cannot see it from the outside. When we get close to it, they will do a quick security check and then open it for us."

Kimble butted in, "Jeez, Josie. You really should pay more attention when we train. You should have been able to sense the barrier."

I asked, "Oh, you can sense barriers?"

She explained, "You can too. You can sense anything that has spiritual energy. I do not care if it is a spiritual attack, a barrier, a spirit animal, or simply another person with considerable amounts of spiritual energy passing you by. You should be able to tell. I can feel shifts in spiritual energy as small as a micro-organism and as far as Rallem."

I was surprised at the intensity of her senses; it was amazing. Kimble was a mysterious fox. I wondered just what the extent of her powers was. I nodded and the conversation ended there. I focused hard after that and was able to feel the barrier and as we got closer to it.

Within a few minutes, we had passed through the barrier and docked in Mallishrine. It was a giant temple, the largest I had ever seen. I was amazed at the sight of it. Malachi told us, "Okay, we have the rest of the day to stock up a week's worth of supplies. I will give out assignments momentarily, but please keep in mind that there is little time for sightseeing, horseplaying, or anything of the sort. We need to hurry if we are to stay on schedule. Now, let us get this over with. Josie: food and cleaning supplies. Johanna: rope, matches, and ink. Kai and Cal, I assume you two do not have an issue with staying close to Josie. She will need help carrying things and even though Mallishrine is safe, I would prefer she has an escort. I must take Kimble to make it to and from the main hall on time, I want to have a quick meeting with the elders while we are here."

We all nodded in agreement, as usual. But Kai and Cal took a moment to speak to Malachi, thanking him for entrusting me to them. Malachi responded harshly saying, "Do not make me regret it, please. She is like my sister and I do not know what I would do if anything happened to her." I suppose he was not used to having to leave me in someone else's care. Up until a week before that, he had seen to my safety himself.

They both nodded, slightly intimidated by Malachi. Then, we headed into town. We had an enjoyable time but the day passed by quickly. When we all met back up on the boat, Malachi was acting strange. I wondered what he spoke to the elders about, but I figured it was not any of my business. I just asked him, "Malachi, are you okay?"

He said, "Yes, Josie, I'm fine." But he was shaking. I just hugged him. I did not say anything else. I just held him. Malachi began to cry. I just continued to hold him, but at that moment, his tears were making me want to cry too. It was heartbreaking to see him like this. I did not like it one bit. I had a bad feeling about it. I was concerned about him, about us. If he were to fall apart, we all would. I did not know how to help him, so I just held him. Eventually, he calmed down and apologized for being so upset. He promised he would explain soon.

After that, we went to bed and the following morning we set sail again. For the long week to follow, we continued to sail, and I watched Malachi closely during that time. He was still acting weird, but he seemed a little better. We were about a half of a day out from Oceanica when Malachi pulled me to the side and said, "I'm ready to talk."

I sat down with him and said, "Okay, well, I'm here to listen."

He sighed and said, "True Princes of Tendu are unique. We are only half-human. It started in the day of the first king and queen of Tendu. He was the head of the fire hound demons, she was a human, they fell in love and established Tendu as a kingdom. Ever since then, each generation of my family has been with a fire hound. It is a proud tradition. The only issue is that now my nature drives me to breed with a fire hound, but my heart drives me to love Johanna. Since demons are instinctual, when I fight my instincts, my demonic aura starts to take over. I asked the elders how to control it, but they did not have an answer. They want me to stop fighting it and let Johanna go. If I were to lose control, it would spell destruction."

I smiled gently. "Do not let her go. You will not lose control; I will not let you. And eventually, your demonic instincts will subside and you will retrain them. I know you will."

Malachi replied, "Thank you, Josie. Promise me something, though, okay?"

"What is it?" I asked.

"If I lose myself, stop me, even if you have to kill me. If you can promise me that, I can love Johanna and try to make it past the other half of myself."

I replied, "Malachi, no. Listen to me, I will tell you how to fix this. It is far simpler than you realize. Truth be told, your instincts do not want you to love a demon. They want you to love Johanna. Do you want proof? Release your demonic energy so it has control of your consciousness."

He said, "Josie, I could never. It is too dangerous."

I got stern with him. "Malachi, I said to release it. Now."

He did. I saw the change in his demeanor as the demonic energy took control of his consciousness. A mischievous smirk covered his face and he slouched. His bloodred eyes widened as if he was on alert. Flames gathered in his hands and he stood on guard, I could see his fear as clear as day. He felt vulnerable and acted aggressively in an attempt to cover for it. I said to him, "Malachi, do not try to fight me out of fear. I am the Priestess Josella and I will destroy you if you become a threat."

He grunted, "What do you want, girl?"

I explained, "You have two options. You can show me your true instincts willingly, or I can force it out of you?"

Malachi's demonic side was stubborn and he refused, so I went and trapped Johanna in a spirit bubble. I said, "The truth now or I will suffocate her in there. I can remove the air easily."

He scoffed, "You wouldn't kill her; she's your best friend."

I chuckled. "You underestimate me." I removed the air from the bubble little by little. I saw Malachi become stressed as he watched her struggle for air.

He called out, "Do not! Stop! Let her breathe! I love her! I admit it, Josie. I love her. Even as a beast that she could never love in return...."

I chuckled and said, "See. Your instincts tell you that she does not love you, not that you do not love her. My advice is that you stop running and act like a man. Get over yourself. Oh, and by the way, I never would have killed her. This was all an illusion. You should have a talk with her, though, the real her, not the illusion I created to make you face the truth."

He nodded and his demonic energy dissipated. His human consciousness took back over and he. Malachi admitted it was time he and Johanna settled things, but our priority then was to make it to Oceanica and we did after another week. It was time to find the last member of our team. The team was ecstatic as we all stood on the dock preparing for what was to come. Little did we know, no amount of preparation would suffice for what was about to happen in Oceanica. We would soon find out that the last member of our team would be the Oceanic Prince, Malachi's worst enemy and cousin, who was half-angel, as Malachi was half-demon.

9

As we walked down the dock and towards the town, a carriage pulled up to us. I heard Malachi scoff when it did, but then, a very obnoxious and eccentric man stepped out of the carriage. "Malachi!" he exclaimed. "And friends too, of course." He looked over at us, and I got the impression it was more that he was estimating me. "My family and I have great news for you." He paused momentarily, then got kind of dark as he said, "If you would like the support of the royal family in Oceanica, which I remind you that you desperately need if you are to accomplish your mission, I will be your new teammate. Got that, demon boy?"

Malachi immediately lost it, which I do not blame him for, the man was an ass, "Jameson, you pompous lunatic? Who do you think you are speaking to me in such a way? I am a true prince of Tendu and I care not for your half-angel blood. I would sooner die than allow you to join my team."

The man named Jameson laughed harshly. "That can certainly be arranged, demonic filth." Then he calmed down some. "However, it will have to wait for another time, my mother and father would like to speak with you at the palace."

"Whatever," Malachi scoffed. "Let us go, team, into the carriage, now!"

We all remained silent throughout the ride, unsure of what to say or do. I had never seen Malachi so angry before. Then again, I could not believe that man had the nerve to speak to Malachi the way he did. I looked over to Johanna to see how she was taking everything, from what I could tell, it was not well. The expression on her face made me think she could haul off and punch this Prince Jameson at any moment. I could not let that happen. As much as he angered me, this man was heir to the throne of one of the most powerful kingdoms on the planet. Perhaps only Tendu could be called it is equal. We needed his support no matter how much we hated the situation. I resolved myself to speak to her, Malachi, and this man Jameson individually as soon as I possibly could. For now, though, my focus needed to be on the meeting with the king and queen.

As we approach the castle, Jameson began to speak. He said, "Welcome to Oceanica, my new friends. I hope you enjoy your stay at our home here. We have prepared our best chambers for each of you. Of course, we have done our research, so Kai and Cal, your chambers are connected to the Lady Josella's so you may come and go as you please. I must ask that on arrival each of you take some time to rest, shower, and ready yourselves for a dinner with the king and queen tonight. Please be sure to dress appropriately, otherwise, you will be turned away and the king and queen have been clear that they would like all of you to be in attendance. If you need guidance, I am sure the Lady Josella has plenty of experience with formal society and how to behave. Tendu's Prince, however, has never actually lived as a prince so I am unsure his title means much in way of experience. I do wonder why a proper lady such as Josella would be traveling with such riffraff, perhaps she was forced to by her parents, just like I am being."

I finally decided to speak up, "My dear Prince Jameson, I apologize for being so forward when we've only just met, but may I speak freely for a moment?"

Jameson nodded, "Of course, you may, my lady. Please, do not hold back anything."

"While I understand that you and Malachi had quite the history, I have come to know Malachi rather well. He is, in fact, a good man and far from anything resembling a true demon. Secondly, any man who has been raised in proper society, such as yourself, has been taught to set his emotions aside when dealing with affairs of state. I am but a woman and I know that. You insult your king and queen by behaving in such a manner in front of guests, and especially not just one, but two women. Finally, I would like to point out that rather than criticizing Malachi's lineage, it may do you some good to get to know him and learn about what he is trying to accomplish. Going into this blinded by a childish rage would make you ignorant and a fool, two things a proper man should never be."

Jameson paused for a second, then smiled mischievously. "You truly did speak freely. You are correct, my lady. I have behaved inappropriately and for that, I apologize. I will be sure that Malachi and I can settle our affairs in private. Thank you for correcting my behavior."

A few minutes later, we arrived at the royal palace. Oceanica's palace was far larger than any I had seen before; it was as if they needed to reinforce their power with their wealth and status. I started to wonder if the royal family of Oceanica was in some sort of trouble. I figured that was not the best moment to inquire, though. We were escorted to our chambers promptly after we arrived. Since we had so much time until we met with the king and queen, Kai and Cal came over to my chambers. Upon entering, Kai said, "This is cool, it makes it really easy to get to you."

Cal nodded and said, "The bed is big enough that we can both lay with you too. Tonight, will be a good night."

"I'm not so sure about that," I replied. "I am awfully glad to be close to you two, but I am concerned about Malachi and Jameson. There is a lot going on here, more than we are being told, and I do not intend to let them continue acting this way without giving us a complete explanation."

Kai and Cal both smiled in an adoring manner as Kai said, "Josie, if something was going on with us, you would want to help us too, right?"

I nodded. "Of course, what kind of question is that?"

Then Cal asked, "I don't really know how to ask this without seeming, I don't know, wrong, but would you want to help us more than you want to help Malachi?"

I was confused as I replied, "More? I would not say more. It would be different, for sure. What is this about?"

The two of them looked at each other and sighed, then Kai explained, "It is just you are so nice to everyone…"

And Cal continued where he left off, "…and it is hard to tell sometimes if you care about us in a separate way than you do other people, or if you are just being nice?"

I began to laugh uncontrollably. "Boys! Kai, Cal. I care about you two in a most unique way. The two of you have my heart. The others are my friends, most definitely. But you two are essentially a part of my soul. I do not know how else to say it."

They each rested their heads on opposite sides of my lap and Cal muttered, "We love you too, Josie."

Then Kai mumbled, "Yes, we do."

I looked down at them and they looked so peaceful. As if all was right in the world, or at least in their world. Maybe Johanna was right and, in some way, the fact that I love them both made them feel better. There was no stress on their faces, no fear, it was nothing like it was a few weeks ago, they felt safe with me now. It had always just been the two of them, but I guess now it is the three of us. Something told me that we were not separate anymore.

We soon began to prepare for our meeting with the king and queen. It was odd, I had not worn formal attire in a while. It reminded me of being back home. I tried to hide my semi-nostalgic thoughts for the event and help everyone prepare. I was the only one who was accustomed to these types of settings. I helped the boys choose cuff links and made sure their suits and ties were on properly. Then I helped Johanna with her corset and dress, then her hair, makeup, and shoes. I barely had time to get ready myself, but I managed. We all met in the corridor afterward to head to the dining hall, Malachi nearly fell apart when he saw Johanna. However, he did find the strength to say to her, "You look breathtaking." She smiled and thanked him.

When we approached the dining hall, the guards and butler quickly examined us. The guards to make sure we did not have weapons, the butler to make sure our attire was appropriate. Then, we entered the room. We stood by our chairs, which had been clearly assigned by name cards until the king and queen were announced by the scribe, he called out, "His Royal Highness, King Bertrand of Oceanica and his queen, Her Royal Highness, Queen Hellen of Oceanica." Then they entered the room arm in arm. The queen immediately began to speak. "I apologize my dears, I am Hellen. I told them not to make this so formal, but no one ever listens, not even to a queen. Have a seat. And Malachi, my dear boy, I have not seen you since you were thirteen years old. How are you? You seem to have grown into a fine young man."

Malachi laughed. "I am good, Aunty Hellen. How are you?"

"I am well, my child. Now please, tell your friends to relax. There is no need for formalities here. Your cousin will be here momentarily. He should be just getting back from his ride," she explained.

I could not help but feel shocked. Malachi and Jameson were cousins. They looked nothing alike and they hated each other so much. I never would have realized if I had not just heard the queen say it. The king said, "So, you must be Josie, I have heard a great deal about you. My son told me you saw fit to silence him earlier, so I am glad there is someone capable of keeping him in check on this team."

I answered hesitantly, "Thank you for your high praise, King Bertrand. But I must apologize as well. I spoke out of turn to your son earlier and I knew better than to conduct myself in such a manner. I simply wanted to defend the honor of my friend."

The king laughed. "You were in no way out of turn, dear girl. And please, call me Bertrand. Malachi is my nephew and I love him. I acknowledge my son's rather extreme views when it comes to Malachi and I would have done no differently than you did had I witnessed what had occurred. You see, Malachi has on multiple occasions bailed this family out of trouble and he will be doing so again by accepting Jameson onto this team you are assembling. So, Jameson has simply developed an inferiority complex and thus tries to demean Malachi by demeaning his demonic lineage and praising our angelic lineage. Though, I have explained to him on multiple occasions that demons are far from the way they have often been depicted in today's world.

"The truth is that they are much different in heart or soul from angels, most of the differences are in the type of magic power and appearance, though, some lifestyle differences exist. An angel's lifestyle mirrors closely that of a monk, while a demon mirrors closely that of a philosopher. Demons simply believe that they can do good while still pursuing the things that make them happy, while angels believe self-restraint allows them to put more positivity into the world around them for humans and for themselves. It is a personal choice. I mean, we would not force anyone to be a monk, would we?"

I nodded. "I understand. That makes perfect sense. I just wish we could get Jameson to understand as well."

The king replied, "All things in due time, Josella, or do you prefer Josie?"

"Josie, please."

"Josie, it is, then."

Then the queen asked Kai, "So, you and Cal are romantic partners or friends, or please explain your relationship with each other and with Josie? I will not judge. I simply wish to understand. I have come to find word-of-mouth to be an unreliable source of finding out the truth."

Kai laughed. "It is okay, I understand it might be confusing. Cal and I claimed to just be friends on Nollent because we were close and being from opposite sides of the North and South Nollent conflict, it was not acceptable for us to be close in such a way publicly. People were more willing to see past it if we were platonic, but the truth is, we are not. We have just always cared for each other. Then, we met Josie. We both care for her deeply as well so we decided that two could become three."

The queen asked, "And is the relationship romantic in nature, or platonic?"

Cal looked at me and said, "We're well on our way to it becoming romantic in nature with her, but nothing too intense has happened as of yet."

"Well," the queen said, "I think it is great that you have decided to let Josie into your worlds. But bear in mind that even if she is the only one you two wish to let in romantically, you should continue to expand platonically. You can never have too many friends in a world such as this one."

Kai replied, "Thank you for your wisdom, Hellen."

Then, the king asked Johanna, "You and Malachi are something of a romantic relationship, are you not?"

She paused and looked at Malachi for an answer, then he said, "Someday, perhaps sooner rather than later. As it turns out, I am far more scared of waiting too long and losing her out of the fear that I am not ready than I am of trying and dealing with the consequences."

The king laughed, "That is called being in love, nephew. When you are in love, the consequences are always worth it. When you are in love, you can do far more than you ever imagined, trust me. I choose my queen out of many women and while my parents pressured me to choose the wealthiest, the best lineage, the best title, and all that nonsense, I realized that it was the woman I had to marry. I had to be with her, not her wealth, not her lineage, nor her title, nor anything else. So, I chose the woman I loved. Since then, many attempts to destroy our love have been made. Still, we prevailed. Our love transcends all because, that, is what love does."

Malachi smiled at Johanna. Then, Jameson entered shouting, "This is absolute nonsense! I cannot join that man's team. I can save our family on my own. Have faith in me, Father."

Malachi stood up before the king could even answer, "Jameson, I am tired of this feud between us. I do not want to fight you. My only goal is to help the world we live in. I know your heart, and you want the same thing. Stand with me."

Jameson replied, "I actually don't disagree with you, but I cannot stand with you. I have to protect my family on my own. I have to prove I am worthy as a prince."

Malachi answered, "That's why they want you to join this team, creating peace on a mission like this will show the people your worth."

"No!" Jameson answered. "No, it will not. Standing my ground and not letting them topple my will."

"No, that will show them you're a stubborn fool who is willing to harm them to hold on to power," Malachi explained.

"We shall duel, then," Jameson purposed. "Winner gets their way."

"So be it," said Malachi.

Then, the king interjected, "If you two are going to do this, a promise must be made to me first. Son, if you lose, you will try to let go of this hatred you have for your cousin so you two can work together and better Oceanica and Tendu."

"Agreed, but I won't lose," said Jameson.

With that, we all headed to the palace training grounds. It was a huge dome where they could use their runes without damaging anything else. They each released their runes and then the queen explained, "This will be an all-out match. No rules, no restrictions. The first person unable to fight will lose. As the challenged guest, Malachi will decide if he wants Jameson to have a handicap."

"No," Malachi said. "I won't give him any excuses when he loses."

Jameson laughed. Then, the queen announced the start of the fight. They both began launching attacks at full power. I asked the king, "Isn't Malachi at a disadvantage already? Jameson uses water runes; water puts out fire."

Then, the king explained, "No, you underestimate Malachi greatly. He has the advantage in this fight. You must remember, fire can also evaporate water."

Shocked by what the king was implying, I wondered if Malachi was truly that powerful. I mean, I knew he was great. I just did not know he was insanely powerful, as if this battle would not even require effort. Then the queen came over and said, "Not to worry, sweetheart. If Malachi wanted to, he would kill Jameson with a single attack. We would not have a son anymore. He can win this fight any time he chooses. He holds back a tremendous amount of power to give Jameson a chance to learn; he always has. Jameson still only holds the power of a prince, Malachi however, already holds the power and strategic focus of a fully matured king."

I was absolutely amazed by what I was hearing, so I watched the battle intently, wondering what Malachi would be like at full strength. I could see how Malachi consistently stayed one move ahead. It was amazing. However, Jameson was becoming frustrated and rash. He eventually realized he would not win and launched attacks where Johanna and I were standing, assuming Malachi would simply jump in front of the attack to defend us and he would finally land a hit. However, it set Malachi off. Malachi effortlessly evaporated the attack and said, "To risk, the safety of those who have nothing to do with this is the most dishonorable thing I have ever seen you do. This fight is over." Then Malachi launched one huge attack, an all-consuming ball of fire. It was huge. Jameson could not escape it. I doubted that he could survive it. But he did. Based on what the king and queen had said, Malachi would have to know what Jameson's limits were. He knew Jameson would survive; I am sure.

After the attack hit him, Jameson was incapacitated. He was immediately taken to the palace healer. Then, we all went back to the dining hall. Malachi wanted to discuss something with the team. He told us, "We now have a full team, so I will tell you all the plans. Jameson already knows, my aunt and uncle will have told him. First, we will head to Tendu and I will take back my crown. The royal family that replaced mine has no business running a kingdom. After that, we will have the support of the rulers of Tendu, Pallentine, and Oceanica behind us. Mallishrine will likely shift its support to us quickly once they see our large support and plans to make peace. Nollent and the mainland will be the real challenges, but with the amount of support we will have accumulated, we should be able to unite ourselves. However, the representative teammates will be vital in doing so. Got it?" We all gave a nod. Then, Kai, Cal, and I all decided to go for a walk by the shore before bed. But, while we were walking, we found something interesting. Or should I say, someone?

10

Kai, Cal, and I were walking along the seashore together. It was a beautiful and sunny day, there was a light breeze coming off the water. I took a deep breath. The ocean air smelled of salt. Oceanica had the most amazing beaches in all the five islands. The sand was as white as snow and it was so fine that it did not even stick to your feet as you walked. The water was perfectly clear, and I could see through straight to the bottom when we arrived. I was having the time of my life, laughing, and playing with Kai and Cal. It felt like all the world was at peace as we frolicked our time away, basking in each other's presence. That is when suddenly, I heard Cal call out, "Look, over there! There is someone behind that rock."

"He's right," I said, surprised. "Come on, let's go check it out!"

We all ran over and it was a little girl with pitch-black hair down to her knees. I could see sand matted in it as if she had not bathed in weeks. Her big, brown eyes struggled to stay open, I could tell she had not been sleeping well. She was skinny, as if she had not been eating properly, maybe even as if she had been starved. She also looked sickly. I wondered if she might have caught a cold sleeping outside. I was appalled at her state. I did not understand why someone would let a girl this young wonder around by herself and end up this way. I knew I had to help her when I asked her, "What is your name, little one? Are you okay? Where are your parents?"

She mumbled, "Lilly." Then, she fainted in my arms. I turned to Kai and Cal shocked at what I was seeing. I could not believe that anyone would leave a little girl like this. I mean, if we had not found her, she might have died. I started to become frantic. "We have to help her, we have to help her now." I called for Kimble and she rushed us back to the palace so I could get the girl medical care. Kai and Cal were as infuriated with her state as I was. The healer told me, "She will be fine, my lady. She just needs to rest for now. I will send for you as soon as she wakes."

I nodded then gave the healer some extra coin as a sign of my gratitude. I waited anxiously for news about the little girl named Lilly when I returned to my chambers. Cal said, "Who would do this? Why is that little girl like this?"

Kai sighed. "I do not know, man. I just do not know. If I did, I would probably kill whoever did it."

I shook my head. "Death would be too easy. Torture for the rest of eternity is more like it. Out of curiosity, what do you two suppose we do with this little girl once she is recovered? The last time I checked, no one on the team has experience raising children."

Kai replied, "She seems to like you. After all she has been through, is it really fair to leave her if she feels attached?"

Cal added, "I mean, it is up to you, Josie. But for once this is not a game, this is a little girl. You cannot just give her away because it is inconvenient to keep her around. If you decide not to keep her with us, let it be because you genuinely believe she will be better off."

I nodded. "You two are right, I completely agree. You know, you two are both great guys. It is rare to see men with hearts like yours. I just want you both to know that I see it and that I value it, but most of all, that I would never betray or do anything to harm the vulnerable sides of you because I know I am the only person you have let get close enough to see."

Cal's eyes widened, as if he was shocked that I had noticed how great a guy he was, then he simply smiled. Kai chuckled a bit, then patted Cal on the back saying, "Yes, we are pretty great, all three of us. Why don't we go meet up with the others now?"

Cal nodded, "Yes, we should get our minds off Lilly. There's nothing we can do until the healer sends word for us."

I agreed and so we headed off. When we got to the lounge, the rest of the team had already gathered there and was awaiting our arrival. They were all sitting in a circle quietly; it looked awkward. We went over and tried to start up a conversation, but no one was really into it. Finally, Jameson said, "I am sorry, okay? I just wish I could be more of a prince, like you, Malachi. You are always saving the day."

Malachi smiled gently and looked down. "You think I am the hero? I am never doing it alone. These people you see around me are the heroes. Josie is the hero, she chose Johanna, Cal, and Kai for the team. The only thing I did right was choose to put my trust in her and then to trust the people she chose. The thing you need to learn is to build a team of people, friends, that you can trust and who will help you to accomplish even the loftiest ambitions. I set out to change the world. Alone, I would surely fail. But with these people beside me, I really feel like I can do it. You should try connecting with people, Jameson."

"I'll give it a try," Jameson said. "I want to be a good ruler and if I am speaking honestly, as I believe you are, I think what you are trying to do is exactly what this world needs. So, I will give you my full support as a member of this team, as promised. And I hope you all will accept me, not only as a teammate but as a friend and ally."

I nodded; Kai and Cal did too. But Johanna said, "My trust is something you will have to earn after the way you have treated Malachi. The first thing you need to learn about friendship and connecting with others is that the person who wishes harm on the one you care for is an enemy. We protect each other. That much is written in stone."

Jameson nodded. "I understand, Johanna. I am grateful that you care about Malachi so much. I looked up to him a lot when I was younger. I guess the line between idolizing someone and being jealous of them was thinner than I realized. I do not know when it started, but at some point, I started to feel like Malachi was this unattainable goal and that everyone wanted me to be more like him instead of just being me. All I really wanted was to come into my own."

Malachi smiled. "You will. And trust me, we all have someone we consider an unattainable goal. That person is what motivates us to keep growing. My little brother is about thirteen now. You are two years older than him, just like I am you. I always thought you would be his unattainable goal."

Jameson laughed some. "I would gladly. Out of curiosity, Malachi, who was your unattainable goal?"

"Your father. You will understand when you are finally ready to train with him. Even now, I would probably lose," Malachi answered.

Jameson looked astonished. "He's *that* strong?"

Malachi was confused as he answered, "Jameson, you do know your father is the most powerful of the five leaders, right? My father is second. Then the Chief of Pallentine. After that, Nollent's King Herrald. We have no clue where Mallishrine's head monk falls on the scale because he does not engage in battle unless it is wartime and there has not been one in this lifetime."

"Wow, I had no clue. When was this decided?" Jameson asked.

"Every year, the five of them gather for the leader's summit. After, they have battles, kind of just for fun, kind of to judge each other's strength," Johanna explained. "The Chief told me about it."

Kai added, "Yes, they are all pretty close to their nearest ranking, though, aren't they?"

Cal nodded. "Except for the Chief and the top two. The gap is unbelievable. The water and fire kings are barely human. Apparently, the water king just barely manages to defeat the fire king every time. But either of them could destroy any of the others with ease."

Malachi laughed. "You all do know my father is not the king, right? He is only invited to those battles because the other leaders like my family more. The actual king attends the summit. No one has ever told him. But, yes, the truth is, we are not legitimate royalty anymore. That will change soon, though. I will save Tendu from those ridiculous fools."

Jameson hopped in, "Yes, the 'real' king if that is what you want to call him is nothing but a greedy, power-hungry, lazy, arrogant fool. There is no doubt Malachi and his family belong on that throne. Differences aside,

Malachi is far more a king than that lunatic will ever be. What kind of king slaughters his people and watches them starve day in and day out? He is destroying the once mighty and proud Tendu! We cannot allow it!"

We all got fired up, and I jumped in, "We'll save Tendu, I swear it."

Johanna did too. "Yes! I would give my all to it!"

Then, it was suddenly like we were a real team. It was great. We had made peace with Jameson. Soon, we would leave Oceanica and head for Tendu, where we will begin our plans to unify the islands, the mainland, and create peace. It was terribly exciting. Soon after, Kai and Cal escorted me back to our chambers. It was time for us to settle in for the night. Kimble lay at the foot of the bed and each of them on opposite sides of me. I still had not heard anything about the little girl, and I was concerned about her. I guess the boys started to notice I was worried because they interrupted my thoughts. Kai asked, "Josie, can we try something?"

"What is it?" I asked.

Cal smiled. "We each want a kiss."

I gulped. "Okay…." And I held my breath as Cal slowly approached my lips. My eyes were closed and I could feel my palms become sweaty as I got increasingly nervous. It was as if the entire world around me had frozen while I waited for that first touch. Then, I felt it. His soft, gentle lips intertwined with mine. As his hand caressed my face and neck, my mind was going crazy. I felt Kai's strong but gentle grip on my waist as he pulled me away from Cal and slowly towards his lips. When they locked, it was as if an explosion of passion had occurred, I felt a rush like nothing I had ever felt before. How could everything go from frozen to this chaotic speed so quickly? I loved it. Both of their hands lingered on my body as the kiss came to an end. I bit my lips and took a good look at each of them.

Kai asked me, "Did you like it?"

I nodded, still speechless from what I had just experienced. I could still feel their gentle touches beaming through my body like lightning. The sensation was bliss.

Cal said, "It was the most amazing experience of my life."

Kai nodded. "I'd like to do that a lot more."

I nodded. "Anytime...."

Then, Jameson came bursting into my room abruptly. Slightly caught off guard by seeing the three of us lying together, he stumbled over his words. I assume it was because he was not as accustomed to the idea of it as Malachi and Johanna. They have had more time to adjust to it. He said to us, "I apologize for the intrusion. Umm, I came to get you. The healer. The girl has woken up."

All three of us immediately got up from the bed and ran through the halls to the little girl. When we got there, I paused at the door. I took a deep breath and opened it gently in an attempt not to startle her. I sat at the girl's bedside while Kai and Cal stayed in the doorway. I asked her, "Hi there, your name is Lilly, right?"

She nodded but did not speak. I continued asking questions until I could get her to speak. "Are you feeling better, Lilly?" Again, she nodded. "Okay, that is a relief. You were not doing too well. What happened to you? Will you tell me?"

She looked around for a moment, then asked, "Are you nice?"

I nodded. "Yes, Lilly, we all are. You are safe here. I want to help you, but I can only do that if you tell me what happened to you."

She replied, "I will tell you. But please, promise me I will not have to go back there?"

I nodded. "You do not have to go anywhere, Lilly. You can stay with me so long as you want to. That is my promise to you." I looked back at Kai and Cal as I said it, realizing that the answer had come to me. This little girl was not going anywhere if she did not want to, not while I was around to take care of her. They smiled, so I assumed they were happy with my decision.

She nodded. "Okay."

Lilly took a slow, deep breath and said, "My full name is Lilliana Nichole Venicia. I am eight years old and until about a month ago, I was the daughter of Lilliana and Norman Venicia of Mallishrine. But my mother and father cast me out so now I am all alone."

Unable to believe what I was hearing, I asked her, "Lilly, why would your parents cast you out?"

"The Venicia family is known for their inexplicable ability to produce children that can reach total enlightenment by the age of five. As I said, I am eight years old and I have not reached total enlightenment. What is most disappointing is that I was supposed to be the greatest of us. I have been able to speak to spirit animals since I was born so it was assumed that I would have immense spiritual power." As she explained, I wanted to cry.

I replied, "That's nonsense, you know? How could anyone possibly learn with such pressure on them, especially a child?"

Lilly scoffed. "The pressure was not the worst part of it, the training was. They would force me to train for days without food, without water, and without rest. I would be beaten when I failed and constantly criticized, even when I succeeded."

"That is horrible. So, what made them finally cast you out?" I asked.

She answered, "The instructor they had hired told them I would probably never reach total enlightenment."

I was shocked. I looked back at Kai and Cal who were still standing in the doorway. They were lost for words as well. Next, I asked Lilly, "And what happened after you left?"

She shrugged her shoulders. "Well, I wandered the streets of Mallishrine looking for help for a while, but to no avail. I was treated as a pest, no different from a rat. No one would offer me food or shelter. I realized that if I stayed on Mallishrine I would surely die."

"So, what did you do?" I asked.

"I snuck onto a trade ship," she explained. "I had no clue where it was going or what I would do when I got there, but eventually it docked in Oceanica."

I sighed, "And why didn't you come to the authorities immediately when you arrived here?"

She looked down and tensed up. "As I was trying to sneak off the boat a man found me. He told me that nothing in life was free and then did the unspeakable. I tried to get away, but I could not."

I began to tear up slightly as I asked her, "Lilly, when you say, 'the unspeakable,' are you telling me this man touched you in an intimate manner?"

She nodded hesitantly.

I asked her, "Lilly, can you describe this man to me?"

She replied, "He was tall and a bit muscular from working on the ship. He had no hair and there was a scar on his cheek in the shape of the crescent moon. It looked as though he had been cut there. He might have been about thirty or thirty-five-years-old."

I turned to the boys and said, "Please inform the king and queen. Tell them that I request that they send out guards to find and arrest that man immediately. I want him in a dungeon for the rest of his days."

Kai and Cal nodded, then ran off.

I turned back to Lilly and said, "Lilly, that man will never hurt you again. Go ahead, tell me what happened after that?"

She continued. "I was scared, so I decided I would just walk along the shore. Whenever people came, I hid. I was out there a few days and I remember being hungry and tired. I guess by the time you found me, I had run out of energy."

I was frozen, what a strong little girl she was. I knew I had to continue to take care of her. I closed my eyes and summoned Kimble through our spiritual connection. She came running down the hall to me. When she got into the hospital, I said, "Kimble, this is Lilly. Lilly, this is Kimble. Kimble is a spirit fox. She is my familiar. I am going to have her stay by your bedside for a while to keep you safe, okay?"

"Yay! Hi, Kimble, can we be friends?" Lilly seemed happy as she began to talk to Kimble.

"Of course, we can be friends, Lilly. You seem like an extremely sweet girl," Kimble replied as she glanced over at me. Her look was one of confusion, though it seemed to be a good kind of confusion. She seemed convinced Lilly was special. I had the same feeling. It was odd, but Lilly's spiritual power was indeed great. With proper training, she should easily surpass most. However, I knew Lilly would not be ready to train for some time. For now, I just wanted her to be a kid, not a priestess. It would be good for Kimble to stay close by her for now, though, a child with that much power could become a target. This way I always have a lifeline to her.

I said to the maid, "Please prepare a meal for this girl. Be sure it is something easy on her stomach. Also, I would like guards posted outside this room until further notice. Anything she needs, you should give to her. Check on her every hour. If anything happens, notify me immediately. Monitor her for signs of illness. No one is to see her besides the royal family, my team, and you. That includes the other maids. Do you understand?"

"Yes, my lady," the maid replied.

Then, Kai ran in, "Come quick. We got him."

I ran through the halls and into the courtyard with Kai. I saw two guards holding a man who fit the description Lilly gave exactly. Cal was standing there too. He called over, "What'll we do with this monster?"

I looked at the man closer, then at the guards, and said, "Make sure he stays in that dungeon for the rest of his days."

The man began to beg and plead for his life, but Cal lost his patience and summoned his runes. He held a boulder above the man's head and said, "You rot as she said, or you die now as I say. Either way, your life is over."

The man gulped and agreed to be taken to the dungeon. Then, Cal stomped off. This was not like him. I was angry too, but his reaction was different. It was as if he had been through the same thing Lilly had. Just as I thought it, I realized. I took off after Cal immediately. He was crying in our chambers. I went in and fell at his feet. I said to him, "Cal, I am so sorry. I did not know. This must be really hard for you."

He lifted me and held me close to his chest. "You wonderful, wonderful woman. You have nothing to apologize for. Kai does not even know. It was my father when I was around Lilly's age. Trust me, she has it worse here. It is hard to deal with when you are a kid."

I hugged him tighter. "I am so sorry. What an evil man? You know, Kai told me about your father before? It sounds like he had done terrible things to you on more than one occasion. He was genuinely a horrible person and I hate it. I hate that I was not there for you back then. Anything you need, tell me, okay?"

He replied, "Just do not tell Kai. Let this be between us, okay?"

"Of course," I said, not realizing what the repercussions would be until much later.

After that, all of us met up in Lilly's room to have dinner. I introduced Malachi, Johanna, and Jameson to her. We all laughed and talked for a few. Then, we got down to business. Malachi said, "The maid said you would be okay to travel, Lilly, so we are going to be heading out tomorrow. Are you coming with us?"

Lilly nodded.

Malachi said, "You heard the girl, everyone. Tomorrow, we sail for Tendu. Tendu is not far from here, so within a week, the battle for the throne will have begun. Be sure that you set your affairs in order before that, I know I will." He looked at Johanna as he mentioned setting his affairs in order. He had come to realize that it was time to make his move.

Everyone headed out, but I stayed for a little to put Lilly to bed. She asked me, "Josie, will you stay here until I fall asleep?"

"Of course," I replied as I sat at her bedside. I looked at her as she drifted off. Once I was sure she was sound asleep, I kissed her forehead, pet Kimble one last time, and decided to head back to my chambers to talk to the boys. But when I arrived, they had broken out into a huge argument. I was not sure what it was about then, but it was not how I pictured us spending the night.

Kai looked over at me and said, "You two are keeping secrets from me now? Am I still part of this relationship because I feel like I am not?"

I answered him, "Kai, what are you saying?"

He asked me, "If you had to choose between us, could you? If so, who would it be?"

"I'm not answering that, Kai," I sighed. "I am not getting pulled into this argument with you two. Settle it yourselves. I will sleep alone, I guess."

They both looked at me as if they were lost, suddenly, they both began screaming at me. Somehow, this is now about me. What did I do wrong? It is not a big deal, right? I just did not want to argue so I figured they could sleep in the other room. It is just one night. I eventually grew tired of the drama and decided to take a late-night walk through the town. While I was walking, I noticed someone was following me. I tried to get away, but they just kept chasing me. Eventually, they grabbed me and put a sack over my head. I tried to fight, but it was no use. I had been kidnapped.

11

They took me to a barn and removed the sack from my head. I struggled but ultimately could not free myself from the ropes and chains they used to bind me to the post. I considered using my spiritual connection to Kimble to alert her, however, who could she tell of my situation? No one else could speak to spirit animals. Then, I remembered that Lilly also had the ability to speak to her, I had to have her get Lilly to tell everyone what had happened to me, and I had to do it quickly. I heard the men talking outside but could not make out the content of the conversation. I wished that I could have so I could relay information about their motive, identities, and possibly even our location to the others. But it was no use, so I began to focus my concentration on reaching Kimble.

I was struggling to make the spiritual connection to her because I was frantic. I needed to calm down. I took deep breaths and closed my eyes. I tried to picture a happier place. I did everything I could to unblock my spiritual power, but it was not working. Then, I realized that it may not be the kidnapping blocking me. It may be the argument with Kai and Cal. I feared I may never get to speak to them again. I did not want our last words to one another to be ones said in anger. In those moments, I felt a release as I swelled up inside with determination to reunite with Kai and Cal, as well as with the others. Finally, I could make the spiritual connection to Kimble.

When our souls finally connected in the spirit world, I said to her, "Kimble! I am so happy to see you right now. Tell Lilly to tell the others that I have been kidnapped."

Kimble asked me, "I understand the situation, I will notify them immediately. Are you hurt?"

"No," I told her, "just scared."

"Okay," she replied. "We are coming, Josie. I promise. Do you know where you are?"

I replied, "No, unfortunately they put a sack over my head on the way here. I assume it is some sort of barn, though."

She answered, "That is fine. We will figure it out. I must go; we need to preserve your energy in case I need to contact you again. If the situation becomes dire and you are being harmed, alert me right away. This is all my fault; I should have taught you how to use spiritual location tracking. Be careful and please, Josie, come back to us safely."

"It's not your fault, Kimble," I replied. "You would have taught me eventually. There is no way you could have seen this coming. I will see you soon, Kimble. Stay by Lilly's side until I return."

She nodded and then we returned to true locations in the material world.

Then, she woke Lilly and told her that she needed to go tell the rest of the team what had happened because she could not talk to them. Lilly and Kimble then ran through the halls and notified the entire team. They gathered quickly to strategize about how to find me. Kai and Cal were distraught, the same fear that struck my heart struck theirs. They ran out of the castle without meeting with the others, knowing nothing besides the fact that I was in a barn somewhere. Malachi and the others decided to take a more organized approach.

They had little to go on, so it was decided that they and the royal guard would have to raid every barn in Oceanica until I was found, starting with the ones closest to the palace, which was in center city and working outward from there. The raids began immediately after that. They searched all night and well into the day.

Meanwhile, the men who had kidnapped me were beginning to argue. The man who was in charge gave strict orders not to touch me, but some of the others did not like it much. He insisted that I needed to remain unharmed, though. I assumed that he was planning to hold me for ransom. During one of the guard shifts, one of the men was caught trying to have his way with me and the man in charge killed him. It caused the others that sided with him to attempt to overthrow him. Naturally, I hoped it did not work out. I hoped he would remain in charge at least long enough for the team to find me. Unfortunately, it did not work out that way. They killed the original leader of the group with a knife to his neck. I saw the blood spill as it covered the barn floor. It was traumatizing. I had never seen a man be killed before. On top of that, the violent men began to form a circle around me and I knew I could not beat them all, but I hoped I could hold them off until my friends arrived. I feared what they would do to me if I could not.

I began to launch spirit attacks at random, but I was still restrained, so it was just enough to keep them at a distance for a few minutes. Then, one of them launched an attack I could not block. I went unconscious. I could not tell you for sure what happened after that. All I know is that I felt different from that day on. Whatever occurred that night changed me. When I woke, I was back at the palace and the clothes I had on belonged to one of the boys. The entire team was at my bedside and Kai and Cal were both crying. Kai said to me, "I am so sorry, Josie. We could not get there in time. We could not protect you."

Cal continued, "We failed you, Josie. This is all our fault. I am so sorry."

I shook my head. "Nothing that happened is on you two. And you boys saved me, as a matter of fact, all of you did. Thank you, I owe you all my life."

Malachi replied, "You owe us nothing."

Johanna continued, "No, we are family. This is what we are here for."

I looked over to Kimble and Lilly and smiled. "Thank you guys especially, I don't know what I would have done without you."

"How did you know I helped?" Lilly asked.

"It was my idea, silly," I answered playfully as I started to get up.

Kai and Cal tried to stop me from standing, I said to them, "Boys, I am okay. Do not worry. Don't we have to get going? We have to get to Tendu, don't we?"

Malachi shook his head. "Josie, sit down." His tone was more serious and sterner than I had ever heard before. "We are not going anywhere today. We can wait another day. Tendu is not going to fall apart before tomorrow. Making sure you are okay is our top priority. Kai and Cal will take care of you for the rest of the day. Johanna will take care of Lilly for you. I will get Jameson and we can make the preparations for our departure tomorrow."

I nodded. "I assume that's an order?"

"You assume correctly."

Then, Johanna said, "Josie, if you need a female to talk to…."

"Thanks, Johanna. I will let you know," I said. Although, I already knew I did not wish to speak about what had happened. I did not even wish to know for sure what had happened. Suspecting was one thing, asking them to confirm was an entirely different. It was best that it is not discussed, at least, not for a long time. Perhaps one day I would be ready, that day was far from it. I thought surely Johanna would understand that.

For the rest of the day, Kai and Cal catered to my every need. I began to get frustrated with it and said, "Boys, stop. Sit down with me. I want to talk to you."

They nodded and sat down, so I continued. "Loves, you both mean everything to me. I want to be with you two. I would never choose just one. It is the three of us until the end of time. I kept the secret because Cal asked me to do so, Kai. I would do the same for you. Just as you would for me and you would both do for each other. We are the team inside of the team. When I was stuck in the barn with those men, I wanted nothing more than to see the two of you. I love you both. Never doubt that again, okay?"

They both smiled as they said, "We love you too, Josie." Then, Kai continued, "Yes, Josie. I am sorry I got angry with you. When Lilly told me what had happened to you, I was so afraid. The thought of never seeing you again was heartbreaking."

Cal nodded and said, "It was truly scary. I do not think we would be us without you anymore. It is just the way things are now. I truly do not remember how we got along without you before."

I replied, "Good, now can you guys please stop freaking out and come lie down with me for a bit? I need to be held."

They nodded, then came to lie with me. In their arms, I felt safe again. I felt as though all the pain of what I had just experienced melted away. That is until I fell asleep and I had a nightmare. The nightmare felt as though I was reliving the whole thing. I woke up screaming and the boys were confused. When the boys asked what was wrong, I told them I needed them to get Johanna. They did.

When she got to the room, I told her what happened. She understood the situation and agreed to explain it to the boys for me. That way they knew what it was if it happened again. She also told me it was normal after what happened and that Kimble may be able to help. Spiritual training helps many women overcome such traumas as it turns out. It was helpful talking to Johanna. The boys came back in a few minutes after she left. They were quiet. It did not seem like they knew what to say. I avoided going back to sleep, though. Then, Kai suggested, "Why don't we stay up tonight, then? We could have a little party, just the three of us?"

Cal smiled. "I think that's a great idea."

I laughed. "I do too. Let us get started."

The three of us laughed, played, and talked for the rest of the night. We had a maid bring snacks and drinks too. Eventually, we all fell asleep. The first thing the following morning, before we had woken up, Malachi came to notify us that something came out when the guards interrogated the men who kidnapped me. They were a part of an assassination attempt by the faction that supports the current leaders in Tendu. The goal was to get Malachi to trade his life for mine. I guess they got word of our plans. Jameson was trying to gather more information on the matter, but that meant that there was a mole somewhere along the lines.

We went to gather with the rest of the team quickly. We all sat in the dining hall waiting anxiously for word from Jameson. When he entered the room finally, his head was down and he was crying. I asked him, "What is wrong? What did you find out?"

He replied, "Mother, how could you?"

The queen's head lowered and she replied, "I am sorry, my son. I genuinely did not mean any harm to anyone. The truth is that I was having an affair and I may have mentioned some sensitive information to the man while I was with him."

"Hellen!" the king said with shock on his face. "How could you?"

"How could I?" she asked "Bertrand, I was forced to marry you. I liked dating you for a while, but I did not want to marry you. When you asked, my parents forced me to because you were going to be king. I never loved you, but I was faithful to you for years regardless. I am sorry, but it is the truth."

"And what? You loved this treacherous man who would bring harm to your son? To your nephew? To Josie?" Jameson asked, then he demanded, "Guards, take her away. Put her in the tower. My father can decide her fate after we leave tomorrow."

Both Jameson and the king were in tears as Hellen was dragged off to the tower. I said to the rest of the team, "We should give them some privacy."

Everyone nodded and we began to leave. Then Jameson said to Malachi, "Tomorrow?"

Malachi nodded. "Tomorrow."

I think Jameson was more determined than ever at that moment. The fact that they were aware that we were coming for them did not make any of us waiver in our convictions. Malachi pulled Johanna to the side after that, he said to her, "I just want you to know, no matter what this battle brings or what happens as a result of it, I love you and I want you at my side."

She smiled as large as life. "I love you too, Malachi, and good, because I'm never leaving."

He took her hand after that and they began to walk through the halls. Kai, Cal, and I all stopped and watched them in awe. It was sweet seeing them together finally. For the rest of the day, we made our preparations. We had the ship loaded with supplies. Kimble and I did some training, Lilly decided to join us too. Kai and Cal trained as well, going hand-to-hand with each other. It was truly an amazing sight. Johanna and Malachi opted to spend their time in a more enjoyable way. They went on a date.

He took her into town to go dancing. They ate and they laughed. He even brought her flowers. Then, he said to her, "Johanna, may I have this dance?" as he put out his hand and bowed.

She curtsied and replied, "I would be honored." As she took his hand and he began to lead her around the dance floor. I could tell they had a truly lovely time when she told me about it. Apparently, he even kissed her in the carriage on their way back. She seemed so happy. I was happy for her. She had waited so long for this. It was great.

Soon, the day came to an end and we all got some rest. The next day, I woke excited, we all did. The time had finally come for us to depart Oceanica. So much had happened here and it was kind of hard to leave. We said our goodbyes to King Bertrand on the docks and then got onto the ship. Then we set sail for Tendu. We were ready for what was to come. Our plans would finally be realized after all our hard work. It was a good feeling, though I must admit, I was a bit nervous.

12

As we sailed for Tendu, we tried to formulate a strategy to take back the throne Malachi's family had lost. Our goal was simple. We were to gain support and take the throne back for Malachi. The murder of the usurpers was not the objective, so if we could avoid it, we would. Malachi thought showing the people the Renki family—unlike the Renugi family—wanted peace would be the best way to gain support. Besides, these people deserve peace. They have been living in chaos for so long, It must be hard.

We decided we would start in the rural area outside of town, where Malachi's family currently lived. Most everyone there supported him already anyway. Once we organized ourselves, we would sweep the kingdom, gaining support along the way. We would probably hit the most resistance once we got closer to the capital area of the town, where the palace and state buildings were. Unfortunately, we would have to get through the royal guard, which was no easy task for a team of eight people to accomplish, especially considering that one of us was an eight-year-old girl and I was not much help in a battle.

I wished that I were more powerful or that I had trained more so that I could be more useful. I felt like I would just be in the way. The others insisted that was not the case, though. Within a day and a half of sailing, Tendu was in our sights.

"We should dock within a half of a day," Malachi said. I wondered what his family was like. He continued, "When we get there, we will head straight for my house. We will need my family's help; they should know if there are any rumors circulating that will be in our interest to know."

"Hey, Malachi," I said, "when we take the throne, you will be king, right? Or will your father?"

He laughed, "No, it will be my throne. My father was the one that told me this is my destiny."

I smiled; I was glad it would be Malachi ruling Tendu. It would be harder to support a man I did not know, at least in the same way. Malachi had earned this. He would be a great king, remembered for generations and loved by his people. I am sure of it. I guess, that also means Johanna would be queen in time. I wondered if she had thought about that at all. I think she would be a brilliant queen. She would be a strong, fierce, warrior queen that had no hesitations when it came to protecting her people or standing by the side of her king. I think that is exactly what a queen should be. Plus, it would unite Pallentine and Tendu in a strong way. Marriage has been used to bond kingdoms since the beginning of time.

When we docked, we headed for Malachi's house. It was not what I expected. Do they really have the true royal family living in a shack? I could not believe it. I mean, how did he afford that boat? His family welcomed us graciously. After we got the formalities out of the way, we sat down to talk. His mother told us, "You all will need to proceed with caution. I do not think you will have much of a chance to gather support prior to going head-to-head with the royal guard, or even the royal family themselves. They have put everything on lockdown in town. They have come to search our house a few times too. I contacted our small support network in town and got word that a lot of information has leaked, orders are to kill you on sight, Malachi. Your fight will likely begin the moment you are seen and it will not end until you win or you die."

Malachi looked around at all of us and after we gave him a nod, he said, "Then, we will just have to win quickly, I guess."

We rested that night knowing that the following day our battle would begin. It was both the longest and shortest night of my life. Each of us was going into this battle prepared to die for our cause, but none of us could have predicted we would lose something much more valuable than our lives. It would be a battle remembered for centuries, maybe even eons to come.

It all started when we hit the gates of the town, as Malachi's mother said, the town was on lockdown so it was under guard. The guard recognized Malachi and immediately called for backup. The guards came rushing at us and with that, the battle had begun. We fought fiercely. Jameson was a great asset against large masses of low-level fire rune users like the guards because they could not evaporate his water, his water just put their fire out. Little did I know, when a low-level fire rune user gets too wet, he or she becomes incapable of using their runes. Unfortunately, the sheer number of the enemy was too much for just Jameson to manage, so we all had to fight.

By noontime that day we had made it about a quarter of the way to the palace. We were doing well. But as we got deeper into town, the resistance we met grew. We could not keep this up indefinitely. We would have to find some way to rest and we would need to do it quickly. Malachi ordered Kimble to go search for a place and to take Lilly with her. I stayed because if she found something I could hear her from a distance with our spiritual connection so she could tell me where to go.

It took about two hours for Kimble to find a solution. When she contacted me, she suggested that I physically bring the entire team into the spirit world. She told me finding a place in the material world was hopeless. I had never brought another person into the spirit world, let alone six. Kimble said she could bring a few, though. She brought Lilly first so she would be safe, then came to meet us to show me how to do it. She asked, "Who do I take?"

I turned to Malachi and yelled, "Who do you want her to take first?"

He replied, "Cal, you go."

I looked back at Kimble and said, "Take him." So, she did. Once I saw her do it, I understood the process, but it was not an easy one. I assumed that Kai would be the next to go so I placed my hands on his shoulders as he continued to battle and I forced a ton of spiritual power into his body. It took a lot out of me. I was not sure how many times I would be able to do it. Kimble and I returned for Johanna and Jameson next. I hoped Malachi could hold his own for a few while we took them. We brought them to the others. Both Kimble and I were out of breath and on the brink of losing consciousness from exerting so much power. We agreed that it would take both of us to get Malachi back here. We went back to the material world one more time and each pushed all the power we could into him, dragging him down to the spirit world.

He said to us as we gathered with the others, "We told you that you weren't in the way, you just saved us all."

I tried to laugh, but I could hardly breathe. I felt as though my lifeforce had been drained. I could barely see. I looked over at Kimble and she looked the same as I felt. I used the last of my strength to reach for her as I lost consciousness. A few minutes later, I woke in a panic screaming, "Kimble! Kimble!" I looked around and Lilly was crying. Lilly said, "Josie, Kimble, she had to leave."

I continued to panic, "What do you mean she had to leave?"

Malachi said, "Your spiritual power, Josie. You were going to die. The only way to save you was to combine herself with you."

"Are you telling me Kimble is dead?" I asked hysterically, but then I heard it, it was Kimble.

She said, "Josie, I am alive. I am just inside of you. I will remain here until your spiritual power accumulates again and then I will rematerialize. Relax, please."

I laughed a little. "Thank God, I thought I had lost you."

She replied, "Well, you did lose something…."

I asked hesitantly, "What did I lose?"

She explained, "This technique is special. The terms of using it are that if I do, I can no longer be your familiar afterward, but you will have even greater spiritual power than ever before. Perhaps even the greatest spiritual power that is known to man because I do not think this technique has been used in over one thousand years."

I began to cry again, but I understood that it had to be done. I replied, "Kimble, just promise me that you will find happiness."

She told me not to worry about her, but I did. Kimble was important to me, she and I had been together for so long now. It did not make sense that we would be apart. I hated losing her. I hated myself for not being strong enough. Why did I put her in a situation where she had to use such a technique to save my life? Why was such a thing happening to me? I was distraught. I continued to cry until I fell asleep. The following day when I woke, Kimble was gone. But I had to keep moving forward. I took a deep breath and said, "Okay, is everyone ready?"

Malachi gave me the signal to go. Then I said, "Everyone hold hands, I want to make this quick." Once everyone was linked, I moved us all back to the material world at once. I immediately began to walk towards the enemy when Kai asked, "Josie, what is this?"

I replied, "I'm not helpless anymore…."

I blasted through the enemy lines with the others and in a matter of minutes, we were standing outside of the palace. The others were amazed at my newfound power, as was the enemy. I felt it radiating through my body constantly. It was like pure energy and with every blast came a blindingly white light. This power was beyond my wildest imagination and I had not even begun to scratch the surface of it yet. I would need to be careful and keep my emotions in check until I could grasp the full extent of it. I took a deep breath as we stood together, when eventually I said, "You guys ready?"

Johanna laughed and said, "Let's get it over with."

Jameson looked at Malachi and said, "It's on you."

Then, Malachi said, "Move out!"

We charged into the castle. Kai and Cal helped me lock all the guards and household staff in the dungeons and stood guard. Jameson got the prince and cornered him in the dining hall. Johanna and Malachi went straight for the king and queen. When they got to the throne room, they were waiting. The queen said, "Malachi, we meet at last."

Johanna interjected, "He is not your problem; I am. Let the men settle this and I will not send you to the depths of hell. That is my one and only offer."

The queen laughed obnoxiously, "Offer rejected, little girl." As she launched an attack on Johanna and they began to fight at full force. Johanna was no weakling, but queens each receive a special blessing from the runes increasing their power when they are wed, thus it would not be a battle easily won. Yet, Malachi was confident that Johanna would win. Blessing or not, the Renugi Queen was no true queen, and regardless of Johanna's bloodline, she had the heart of a queen. The king asked Malachi, "Aren't you going to help your little girlfriend?"

Malachi smiled. "She is not the one that needs help, trust me. Now, let us settle this."

"Agreed," said the king. Him and Malachi launched attacks simultaneously, countering each other and causing a huge explosion. We could hear the battle begin to rage all the way from the dungeons, but as it did, another battle was also starting. Jameson was struggling to keep the prince contained. When we heard battle coming from that part of the castle, I said, "I will go back him up. These guys are locked up, they only need one guard. If the prince gets to the throne room, the battle there will be uneven."

The boys agreed but insisted that one of them come with me. Cal came because he was stronger in battle and those in the dungeons could not use their runes, so Kai would be fine alone. Cal and I rushed to Jameson and once we arrived, the prince settled down. He knew he could not beat us all. Meanwhile, back in the throne room, Johanna had produced a strategy to knock the queen unconscious. During the battle, she used her ability to communicate with nature and animals to call to send a message to Hembron, who then flew by launching attacks at the queen. In her attempt to dodge them, she stopped paying attention to Johanna who quickly walked up behind her and knocked her unconscious with a rock that had fallen loose during the battle. She thanked him then brought the Renugi Queen to the tower because runes could not be used there any more than they could be in the dungeon. Johanna returned to the throne room to watch as we all waited anxiously for word from Malachi.

He was not having such an easy time beating the king, though. The man was not planning to give up the throne without a fight. However, he made one slipup when he launched his attack. He overestimated his ability to control a large attack and underestimated Malachi's ability to manipulate fire that did not belong to him. It was much larger than he could control and so when it became unstable, Malachi was able to take control of it and add all his power to it while launching it back at the king. It was enough to put him out of commission for a long while. We put the king and prince in the tower with the queen quickly after that.

Then it did not take us long to gain the support of Tendu after the battle. It was only a matter of weeks, in fact. Malachi's coronation was set to be in just one more week and the entire island was looking forward to it. Afterward, he would banish the false royals to Pallentine where the Chief would gladly accept them into his tribe as pig farmers that he would keep a close eye on for us. Everything was working out well. But we knew we still had a long way to go before we had completed all our goals, taking back the throne of Tendu was just step two of our master plan, after building the team.

It was funny, I could remember a time that I did not believe in Malachi and what we were doing; then next thing I knew, we were celebrating the completion of this second step and I had been all in for a while. I was not sure what had changed, but I knew that there was nothing else I would rather be doing. Then it occurred to me that perhaps I was the thing that had changed the most on this journey. I was a better person, stronger, wiser, and I had people who genuinely loved me for me that I loved in return. I was not just a spoiled noble girl anymore.

Planning Malachi's coronation was quite the task too, of course. We needed to invite many important noblemen from across all five islands, but also from the mainland too. Malachi put me in charge of that list. We also had to plan décor. Malachi had to practice his speech as well. It was quite the ordeal. Luckily, I had some experience with planning such events and so did Jameson. He and I took the lead on it. It was decided we would invite some of the lower-class citizens of Tendu as well because we wanted them to feel included in the affairs of the kingdom.

When the day finally came for Malachi to be coronated, we spent nearly half the day getting dressed. Of course, the maids were able to help the team dress appropriately for the occasion so Jameson and I did not have to. It was nice because we needed the time to prepare ourselves, plus, I had to get Lilly ready too. Kai, Cal, Lilly, and I finished getting ready just in time to meet the others. We met up with Johanna and Jameson in the throne room, where the ceremony would be held. Unfortunately, we would not see Malachi until he made his official entrance.

Our guests began to arrive one by one. We greeted them graciously and we all began to enjoy ourselves. Everyone was dancing, eating, and drinking when finally, the scribe announced Malachi's entrance by banging his staff twice and calling out, "The true Prince of Tendu, Malachi Le'Roy Tendu." Malachi entered the room in the traditional ceremonial outfit. It was a blood-red robe and a crown of solid gold full of rubies and diamonds. All eyes turned to him and everyone became silent as the orchestra played quietly and he slowly approached the stairs to the throne.

When he got to the stairs, he knelt on the first one. The priest stood above him and put out his hand. Malachi kissed it. Then the priest began to speak. "We have all gathered here today for one purpose: To restore our beloved Tendu to its former glory under the rule of its true ruler, the Tendu family. Malachi Tendu, who kneels before me now, has fought long and hard for this kingdom and its people, so that we may prosper once more. Before I proceed with the ceremony and name this fine young man king, I must ask, does anyone among us have any reason that he should not assume this post?" The priest paused as he waited for a response when there was none, he continued, "Then so be it. Malachi Le'Roy Tendu, do you solemnly swear to give your all to this land? To govern it fairly, justly, and with kindness and love in your heart? To protect its people, its wealth, and all its contents? And to be a symbol of hope for all who see you?"

Malachi solemnly replied, "I do."

The priest continued, "Then, with the power invested in me by the Kingdom of Tendu under the spiritual guidance and truths taught in the Temple of Mallishrine I, Priest Relenti Quazimo, pronounce you, Malachi Le'Roy Tendu, King of Tendu of the Islands of Rune. Please, recite the King's Fire Rune prayer."

Malachi closed his eyes, bowed his head, and said, "I call upon thee, fire runes of the Island of Tendu, lend me thy power."

Malachi began to shine for a moment, the runes responded to him. Everyone was shocked. Apparently, the runes had not responded to a king since Malachi's last ancestor took the throne. It was truly an amazing sight. I felt like I was watching history being made. As it turns out, I was. Malachi taking back Tendu would come to change the world as we knew it. After that, the priest pronounced the ceremony over and Malachi took his seat on the throne. There was a party after. Malachi came to us during it and asked, "How did I do?"

We all laughed and Johanna told him, "You did great, my love. I am proud of you."

He smiled shyly and said, "Johanna, I know it is a bit early for this but now that I am king the pressure will be on me to find a queen and produce an heir. The country needs the security of knowing that I have a successor in the case of an assassination or illness. And honestly, I do not really see the point in waiting anyway, I love you. So, I was wondering if you might consider, well, you know…marrying me?"

Johanna laughed hysterically, "Malachi, of course, I will marry you. I kind of assumed that is what we were doing."

Relieved, Malachi sighed and said, "Oh, good. Well, here." And he put a ring on her finger.

Johanna smiled and we all began to laugh. I ran over and hugged Johanna saying, "Congratulations!" then to Malachi as well. Malachi then continued to announce his engagement to everyone else saying, "Excuse me, everyone! Can I have your attention for just a moment? I would like to give my speech now. First and foremost, I would like to thank you all for joining me tonight. I promise I will be everything Tendu deserves. What most do not realize is that a king is not a ruler, but one who should serve his kingdom proudly. Secondly, I would like to announce another bit of good news for the night. I have chosen my queen. I would like you all to meet my lovely fiancée, Johanna, a strong, beautiful woman from the island of Pallentine who has stood by my side through many trials. There is no one I would trust more with the well-being of my beloved Tendu."

Everyone cheered as Johanna approached Malachi and he wrapped his arm around her waist. Once they quieted, he continued. "Thank you, thank you. I promise you; she will be a brilliant queen. Lastly, I would like to introduce you all to the team I have assembled. They will all be helping us create peace and prosperity by uniting the islands, the mainland, and ending all these ridiculous injustices we are seeing. Of course, Johanna, who represents Pallentine. We also have my cousin, Prince Jameson of Oceanica. Cal, representing Northern Nollent, and Kai representing Southern Nollent. Lilliana, or Lilly, is from Mallishrine. Do not underestimate her, her age means little, she is perhaps the strongest young lady I have ever met. Lastly, is the Lady Josella, or Josie as we call her. She is from the mainland and honestly, I do not think any of us would be here without her. She often underestimates herself, but she truly is the person who brought us this far."

The guests went wild cheering as the entire team stood proudly before them. Finally, Malachi was king and his coronation was coming to an end. We enjoyed our accomplishments that night, but our journey still was not over. Though, we were far closer than we had ever been. The goal was finally within our grasp. With three of the five islands leaders already on our side, it would be much easier to begin making changes. We had come so far from just me and Malachi on a boat hoping that someone would side with us somewhere along the line. We had started a movement that swept all five islands like a tidal wave.

13

The movement was branded "The Better World Movement." Within a week, Mallishrine had shifted its full support to us as well because of the movement's overwhelming growth and its peaceful intentions. Citizens from all over had decided to back us in our attempt to better things. We were still struggling with Northern Nollent and the mainland, though, so Malachi asked me and Cal, "I need you two to do me a favor. Josie, the officials from the mainland are altogether nonresponsive to our attempts to contact them. I need you to go try to reason with them. Cal, the officials from Northern Nollent are responsive but uncooperative. So, I want you to talk to them and see if you can get them to cooperate. Being as though it is unlikely that they will, I will also send Kai with you so if they continue to refuse, you guys can organize our massive number of supporters in Southern Nollent and make them give in. I am thinking you will be able to take Northern Nollent by force if need be. Of course, if aid is needed, Oceanica and Tendu are prepared to send it immediately. We do not want it to become a war, so we want it to end quickly if we have to do it forcefully."

Johanna added, "I spoke to the Chief, and Pallentine will send troops as well if we need him to."

Malachi nodded. "Yes, I figured he would, but I would rather not have Pallentinian troops involved. I would rather focus on the disconnect with Pallentine.

I want to begin arranging social events for both townsfolk and high-ranking members of society where people from different islands can truly come to understand other cultures. The stereotypes will be abolished quicker that way and it will help avoid war. Until then, it is best the Chief support us in a political sense because the movement has caused some high tensions. Our goal is not to take over other nations and kingdoms. It is to help other nations and kingdoms improve relations with one another and build more stable and happy communities for their citizens. By splitting our attentions between Nollent and inter-cultural understanding events, we show people that we are looking for cooperation from these kingdoms, not control."

Johanna smiled. "This is why I love you. You always think things through so well and you are so kind."

Malachi blushed, but then Cal said, "I do not want Josie going to the mainland alone. We all know this mission could be dangerous and if Kai is with me and Kimble is gone, who is with her?"

Malachi laughed. "Josie is now one of the most powerful people on this planet thanks to Kimble's sacrifice. I even question if my or Jameson's father could beat her. I understand your feelings for her, but do not continue to underestimate her or you will land yourself in the most treacherous of positions."

Cal scoffed, "I have never underestimated her, but powerful and invincible are not interchangeable. If she is to go, she will not be going alone. I do not care how powerful she is; she is not immortal."

I smiled as I thought about how great it was that he still wanted to protect me. Then, Malachi said, "Fine, but please, I must insist you heed my warning. Not understanding this could be dangerous, indeed. Josie is like my sister, but she does not need your protection or mine anymore. In fact, we may need hers. I will send Jameson with her. Johanna and I cannot leave here, unfortunately. We have wedding plans to make and I have a lot to do as king right now."

Cal replied, "Then, so be it." Then, he asked me, "Are you taking Lilly with you as well?"

I answered, "I cannot really leave her here. She has begun to look at me as a mother figure and she really needs that kind of positive female figure in her life."

Cal smiled gently and said, "You two be careful, okay?"

I nodded and said, "You guys do the same. I will miss you. We will see each other soon, though, right?"

Cal nodded, "Of course, we will. I promise."

Malachi said, "I will have the maids do the packing and preparations so you guys can say your goodbyes. I will notify Kai and Jameson too; I suspect Kai will rush straight to the two of you when he hears. Should I tell him you will be in the gardens? I can make sure no one else comes there for a while."

I replied, "Yes, please. Thank you, Malachi." Then I said to Johanna, "When I get back, I better not find out you have replaced me as maid of honor. I wish I could be here to help."

She replied, "I would never. And it is okay. I look forward to your return. Promise me you will be careful, Josie."

"I will," I answered, wrapping my arms around her and Malachi. I said to him, "Thank you for having faith in me, Malachi."

Then, I took Cal's hand and we went towards the gardens. We sat there quietly, waiting for Kai. This was the longest the three of us will have been separated since we got close. Kai ran up after we sat down and sat down with us. The silence continued until we all suddenly began laughing, and I said, "What are we being so weird for? We will see each other again soon, right?"

Kai replied with tears in his eyes, "Of course, we will."

Cal said, "Yes, we have nothing to worry about."

Then, we all hugged. We stayed that way for a minute. It was hard to let go. But then Jameson came and said, "Josie, it's time."

I nodded and gave the boys one more good squeeze before heading off with Jameson. They left only a few hours after we did. As I sailed, I thought that they would probably make it to Nollent long before Jameson and I made it to the mainland. I also thought it was kind of weird being alone with Jameson, he and I never really bonded like the others. Then, I pepped myself and decided I would use this opportunity to do just that. After all, he was a member of the team too, and he was Malachi's cousin. I walked over and asked him, "How are you feeling about this trip?"

He replied, "I do not know. I have never been to the mainland before. It would be nice to know more about it before we got there."

I nodded and told him, "Well, the people we will be dealing with are mostly upscale noblemen and possibly royalty. No one there knows about runes or the truth about history to my knowledge. They all think they are better than everyone. You are a prince, so they will likely treat you well. Your family has a lot of trade relations with our land. We depend on you for many of our imports, so they will try to make good with the next king. My parents are surely part of what is blocking our attempts to spread the movement to the mainland. My family is very powerful.

"My father is the First Duke, the only ones above us are the royal family themselves. We are cousins to them. My mother and father probably still hold resentment towards me for rebelling against them and leaving, which is likely the cause of them trying to block our movement. I am sure Malachi knew this, which is likely why he decided to send me. Likely, it was his way of telling me it was time to settle things with them. In the long run, we will need their co-operation if we are to win over the nobles and royalty in the mainland. However, I do not expect it will be easy to get them to cooperate. Though, others may cooperate solely because they do not want to make an enemy of you. Then again, they may also remain neutral or uncooperative because the other option is to make an enemy of my parents."

Jameson sighed. "Reminds me of home; what a pain…. I guess we will figure it out, though."

I nodded. "I always hated the politics of being a noble."

He laughed and said, "Me too. It is like you must jump through one hundred hoops to convince people to do the right thing, even when they know it is the right thing. I will never understand. However, I refuse to be anybody's dancing monkey. I am the Crown Prince of Oceanica, our power is only rivaled by Tendu. A petty vendetta some parents have for their daughter for deciding to live her own life is beneath me and if they wish to continue to act like children then we will treat them as such. I am sure the royal family of your mainland will see me and gladly hear my grievances about them if I threaten to end the trade that allows them to live so well, which trust and believe me, my parents will grant me the power to do if need be."

I laughed hysterically.

After that, the ice was broken and we began to really bond. It was nice to know him and I were on the same page. He really was a prince; he had the same kind heart and fierceness about him as Malachi did. He did not realize it, but he was a lot like the cousin he looked up to so much as a child. It was sweet in a way.

Meanwhile, Kai and Cal had already arrived in Nollent. When they docked, Cal headed to meet with the Northern officials, while Kai went to organize our Southern supporters so they were prepared in case Cal sent word that they needed to attack. When Kai met with the volunteers, he realized that we would need more manpower to stand against the more powerful runes of Northern Nollent. He sent word to Malachi and Johanna via a tradesman from Pallentine who sent the message to Johanna using the trees, requesting that backup be staged off the coast in case it came to a fight. Malachi agreed to send it. He thought that seeing that South Nollent would not stand alone might sway North Nollent to give in without a fight. Within three days, the battleships, which were powered by runes, not just sails, arrived from Oceanica and Tendu. This also inspired more volunteers from South Nollent to join.

It was around that time, that Jameson and I made it to the mainland. We immediately began our meetings with the nobles of the land. It was determined that if we could sway fifty percent of them to our side that the king and queen would hear us out and make a ruling about if the land would officially support us. If we failed, our only option would be to gain support in the village illegally and force them to accept us, which could lead to a fight. We sat around a long table with all the nobles, there was twelve total, which meant we needed a minimum of six on our side to get to the royal family. I hoped Jameson's presence would sway a few, but really, it was up to me to do this.

My father was at the head of the table and my mother stood at his side. I silently prepared myself for what was to come. Then, it began. My father was the first one to speak. "Tell us, why have you come here today, Josella?"

I replied, "Father, you already know the answer to that, I am sure. Our history has been covered up for centuries, our citizens oppressed, our connection with the islands limited to trade, and our culture diminished. We have created a team of representatives made up of myself, Prince Jameson, who is here with me today, King Malachi, Johanna, who will soon be Queen of Tendu, Lilly, who has also joined us today, Kai of Southern Nollent, and Cal of Northern Nollent. We created this team with the sole purpose of bonding each of our lands, sharing in our knowledge and cultures, and creating peace and prosperity for all. We already have support from four of the Islands and their leaders and are soon to have the fifth as half of Nollent has already shifted its support. The mainland must join us as well. It will be better for it. The only other option is to cause the entire land to suffer because you choose to remain stubborn, which the people will in time overthrow you for, especially once they learn they have another option. So, please, hear me today, noblemen. I offer you a chance to side with us willingly and gain favor with your people, thus gaining more power. Or be against us, and them, tomorrow and lose all you have."

Jameson added, "I also implore you to keep in mind that without the trade this land has with mine, the lives you currently live are impossible to continue living. We provide all the delicacies you have, from your foods to your furs. Tendu, Pallentine, and Oceanica are all prepared to cease trade with the mainland immediately if you refuse to cooperate."

My father scoffed, "You lie! The people would starve, you would not dare!"

I laughed. "We would, Father. We prepared a plan to evacuate the people. Only you nobles and royalty will starve."

The other nobles looked scared, then I said, "I believe it is time to vote."

My father sighed as he realized he had lost and said, "All in favor of sending this to the king and queen?"

All the noblemen besides my father raised their hands. His stubbornness never ceased to amaze me. We were taken to meet the king and the queen after that. They seemed to be nice, but they had quite the stipulation on giving us their official support. The queen said, "I have spoken to my husband and we have decided that if the Prince of Oceanica marries our daughter, we will support you. Of course, we will give you two a few weeks to get to know each other before we formally announce the wedding and begin planning, right, honey?" The king nodded. I was under the distinct impression that the queen was the one running the show here. I pulled Jameson to the side and whispered, "You don't have to do this. We will find another way."

He replied, "No, this is fine. Besides, who is to say I will not like the princess? We are talking about uniting kingdoms, Josie. Marriage was always a possibility, especially being as though a woman cannot take the throne alone. The king and queen have no heir if she does not marry someone with a royal bloodline. Your father would be the next king, or if he died, you would be next in line. Your relationship with Kai and Cal would have to end. You would have to choose one to marry. The alliance would be impossible. This is what is best."

I thought about what Jameson was saying and he was right, without this marriage everything would fall apart. He was the only single, eligible royal left. It was the only way. So, I agreed and he told the king and queen, "Well, let's meet my future bride." He followed the queen to go meet the princess and I went to send word of the agreement to Malachi. I guess we had two weddings to plan now, though I was sure Jameson would not announce his until after Malachi's. That was simply common courtesy. He would likely be stuck here for a few weeks, though, except for Malachi's wedding.

By that time, Cal had also intimidated Northern Nollent into forfeiting as well. They had to give up control of their government, we would install new leadership and recreate their government. Oppression was built into that system. They headed back to Tendu, as did I. Jameson stayed in the mainland with Sonya, the princess, and said he would keep us updated on things and would be looking forward to receiving an invitation to Malachi's wedding. With that, all the nations were on our side. We could slowly implement change across all five islands and the mainland.

14

Things were going great for all of us. Jameson seemed to like the princess he agreed to marry, which was a relief. Kai and Cal had set up a vote so South and North Nollent could elect their new officials as one. Of course, they were elected to remain the team representatives. The first President of Nollent was a man named Hector Kidman. He was from South Nollent and many Northern Nollentines voted for him. They were really coming together. Johanna and Malachi's wedding was only a few days away too. So many people were coming from all around. The Chief, Jameson and Princess Sonya, the King of Oceanica, the new President of Nollent, and even the top Monk from Mallishrine.

Kai, Cal, Lilly, and I also had big news. We planned to tell the team at dinner tonight. Once we all sat down, I got everyone's attention and said, "Excuse me, I have something I want to tell everyone. Well, the four of us do, anyway. We discussed it with Lilly, and she decided that she wants me to officially adopt her. What she does not know is I already have her adoption certificate and she just must sign it. The four of us will be buying a home in Tendu. It is right here near the castle, where we can all live together in peace."

The others clapped for us as a maid rushed a quill and ink over for Lilly to sign the certificate. She looked so happy. It was a brilliant moment. The good news is that it was not just us doing well. All the islands and the mainland had made serious progress as well. Besides Nollent, Pallentine had already improved its relations with other places by an estimate of twenty percent. We wanted to keep improving it, so other nations knew that they were not savage. We wanted others to understand their culture. But the progress we had made so far was great. We would continue holding our cultural learning events.

Oceanica was improving too. Crime rates and poverty were down significantly, as well as in Tendu. Mallishrine brought down the barrier and we implemented a new training program for children, one that would not put so much pressure on them. We also created a program to help other children on the island in situations like Lilly's. The true history was being taught in the mainland now and the wealthy's nervous and condescending views were beginning to dissipate. We were surely making good progress. It was a happy time.

The day of Malachi and Johanna's wedding finally came. She looked beautiful when we finished getting ready. It was set to be a wonderful day. She said to me before the ceremony began, "Josie, do you think I will be a good wife? A good queen?"

I smiled. "Absolutely. I cannot think of anyone better for Malachi or for Tendu."

She smiled in relief and then it began. Lilly walked down the aisle set up in the throne room first tossing flowers to each side as she stepped to the melody of the music. I followed her, as Johanna's maid of honor. I smiled seeing Malachi looking so nervous at the end of the aisle. Jameson stood by him as his best man, Kai, and Cal too as groomsmen. They looked great. Once I reached the end of the aisle, I waited for Johanna's entrance. She entered proudly, shining like a star. Malachi teared up. It was beautiful.

She reached the end of the aisle and Malachi took her hand. Then, the priest began the ceremony saying, "We have gathered here today to join these two souls. Johanna, before we proceed, I ask you, do you understand that today you are not only swearing yourself to this man, but to this nation? Do you swear to uphold your duties as queen by caring for our king, our country, and our people? And do you understand the weight of the responsibilities you are assuming today?"

She replied, "I do."

Then, the priest continued, "Then, I shall marry you today. Malachi, do you understand that by marrying this woman you are now not just king, but a husband? Do you swear to uphold the duties of such by caring for her and loving her? Do you understand all that this entails?"

He replied, "I do."

The priest continued, "Then, I shall marry you today. By the power invested in me, I now pronounce you husband and wife, and by extension, I pronounce thee, Johanna, Queen of Tendu. May you live long and happy lives. You may now kiss the bride."

Then, Malachi lifted Johanna by her waist and kissed her. They were finally husband and wife, king and queen, just as they should be. Everyone cheered as they sat in their thrones side by side and the queen's crown was placed on Johanna's head. Somehow, the ruby and diamond-studded crown just looked right on her.

Within a week, Jameson and the Princess Sonya had sent out invitations to his wedding. Kai, Cal, Lilly, and I had moved into our house too. Malachi and Johanna were out on their wedding tour, but they said they would come to visit us when they returned. The four of us were enjoying ourselves as we decorated and settled into our new home. Lilly told me, "Josie, can we do my room like the spirit world? I want to feel like Kimble is always nearby."

I smiled and said, "Yes, of course, baby girl. And you know, I bet Kimble is nearby sometimes. She probably comes to check on us a lot. She just cannot let us see her because we miss her a lot and she knows she cannot stay."

Lilly smiled in return. "You are probably right. One day, I want to become powerful enough to have a familiar. Then, Kimble can stay. She will be my familiar."

I teared up. "Who knows? Maybe she will. You will just have to practice until you are strong enough to find out."

Lilly laughed, and then I said, "Okay, you to bed."

"Good night, Josie," she said.

"Night, Lilly," I answered.

Then, I went to my room with Kai and Cal. We talked for a little while, then Kai said, "Josie, I really have to thank you. You changed my life when you showed up."

Cal added, "Yes, thank you, Josie."

I looked down shyly. "No, thank you two. I would have never had the courage to come this far without you two standing by me."

Then, I kissed each of them before we went to sleep. We woke to a surprise the following day, Malachi and Johanna were at our door. Malachi said, "Grab Lilly and come on, we have to meet the team now."

I did not understand, but I did as he said. He rushed us to the palace where the team had gathered urgently. The Chief and Jameson's father, King Bertrand, were there too. Malachi began to explain, "We have a crisis. The alliance is being threatened by an underground group that has begun moving against us. They preach hate but disguise it as love and peace. We need to act to put this group to rest immediately. We need to do it peacefully; we cannot afford to create martyrs."

I asked, "How will we manage it?"

The Chief replied, "We don't know how big the group is, so hunting them down and arresting them might not be possible."

Then King Bertrand added, "Negotiating with people that are trying to overthrow us is never a promising idea."

Kai asked, "Why don't we just shrink them?" We all looked at him, then he explained, "Look, we have the favor of almost all the people. We will ignore them and if we are asked about them publicly, we will minimize them. They are not a big deal. We can refer to them as a small group of people who disguise hate as peace and preach injustice. We can tell people that it is best to ignore them and focus their energy on supporting the positive work we are doing, not the ramblings of a few people."

Malachi laughed. "I like that. It puts a focus on our action versus the fact that they are just talking. It also minimizes them. Does everyone agree?"

We all did, so for a few weeks to follow, we relayed that plan to the rest of our allies and we all acted accordingly. Soon after, things quieted down again.

Malachi warned us to keep listening for rumors of other groups like that, though. They are easier to tackle early on and they will be common for the first year because people will be under the impression that power is still unstable or that there is some sort of vacuum. Regardless, we were all confident we could manage it.

It did not take the four of us long to finish decorating our new home after everything. I was happy it was finished. Kai and Cal seemed a little down, though, I asked them, "What's wrong, guys?"

Kai sighed, "Malachi and Johanna. Jameson and Sonya. It sucks that we can never get married."

I looked down. It is kind of disappointing to me too. I would like to be able to marry the two of them, but no priest would do it and it would cause an uproar. Even with Malachi's permission, the king has no authority over the priests when it comes to religion. Cal finally interrupted my thoughts. "Screw it, I do not care if we can have a wedding or not. From now on I am just going to tell everyone we are married. I do not need some ridiculous ceremony to tell me our souls are joined."

Kai looked up and said, "Yes! You are right, Cal. Same here! We are married and that is that. Are you in, Josie?"

I nodded. "Of course."

Lilly came out from around the corner and asked, "Does that mean I can tell people that you're both my adoptive dads?"

The three of us laughed and said, "Yes" at the same time.

We all laughed and played after that. We were happy together. A week later, Jameson got married to Sonya. She, Johanna, and I did some girl bonding as we helped her prepare for the big day. It was good to get to know her. It reassured me that she was a good person who would treat Jameson well. I guess some arranged marriages do work out. I wondered if she and Jameson would fall in love? Or maybe, they would just be friends that are married? I guess it is really none of my business, so long as he is happy with it, that is.

It seemed we were all going to be moving on to bigger and better things soon. I was not sure what came next anymore, but I knew one thing for sure, the bonds we created between the islands and the mainland, but especially with each other were unbreakable. After Jameson's wedding, it was about a month before we all saw each other again. We would not have if the lands had not deemed it necessary for the representatives to hold a monthly meeting to air grievances and concerns, but also to give updates and maintain relations.

That first month, we would meet in Nollent and then would alternate by the month. Since we were in Nollent, we decided to hold the meeting at the café where I first met Kai. Johanna and Malachi laughed. He said, "I remember we did not want you to join the team back then, but Josie insisted. I have to say, I am sorry. Her instincts about you were right. I could not have chosen better men than you and Cal to be by her side. Thank you both for taking care of her."

"It's cool, my brother," Kai replied. "I have missed you and Johanna, honestly. We have all been so busy. Josie thinks Lilly is almost strong enough to have a familiar now."

Malachi looked over at me. "Really? That is amazing! Do you think Kimble will be her familiar?"

I answered, "If I am being honest, I do not. Familiars are specific to the person they bond with. I think that is something Lilly must find out for herself, though. I have come to terms with it. She needs to find her own bond with the familiar she has, and right now she is simply trying to restore the one I had."

Malachi nodded. "Are you sure you're the same spoiled little noble brat I found trying to ditch her guards on the mainland?"

Cal laughed. "Our Josie? No way!" Of course, I could hear the sarcasm in his tone, so I laughed a little too. I guess some part of me will always be spoiled.

Johanna said, "Josie, I was wondering if you wanted to have a girl's weekend with me at the new shopping center in Oceanica next weekend? We need to catch up."

"Of course," I replied, then asked, "Can I talk to you outside for a moment?"

We stepped out and I said, "You are pregnant, aren't you? Have you told him yet?"

She replied, "I'm planning to tell him in a particular way. That's why we're going to Oceanica."

I nodded and we quickly returned to the group. They had already moved into talking about business. It seemed Jameson had some important news. He explained, "The mainland has another kingdom farther inland; tensions have developed. I am keeping an eye on the situation since I am there all the time, but I just wanted the team to know because if war breaks out, our allies on the mainland might call on us for help. That kingdom allies with others farther inland, and they will not be fighting alone. Our runes will give the mainland the advantage if they are invaded, though. The other kingdoms would not know about them."

Malachi replied, "Tell the king and queen they can rely on the support of Tendu if they are invaded."

Johanna added, "I will alert the Chief as well. Pallentine is closest to the mainland geographically and I am sure he would not mind."

Kai and Cal looked at each other momentarily and Cal said, "Same goes for Nollent, we will make sure they are aware an ally may call on them."

I asked, "Will Mallishrine go to war for an ally, though?"

Malachi shook his head. "I am honestly not sure. Truth be told, they might because I doubt that if our allies on the mainland are invaded, the invaders will stop there. They will come for the islands as well."

I nodded. "Yes, they will. I am sure of it. I will talk to them and try to get them to see that. I have built a relationship with them through the work I have been doing there to help children."

Malachi replied, "Thanks, Josie. I honestly do not think they would be willing to hear anyone else. I am sure they can sense your spiritual strength and respect you as much as the Head Monk, especially seeing as though you are a priestess by lineage."

I nodded.

Johanna asked, "Does anyone have any other business?"

No one did, so we just spent time together a bit longer. Then, we all went our separate ways. We did not hear anything else about the tensions on the mainland until our next monthly meeting.

15

That meeting was at the palace on Oceanica. It was odd because Jameson had not arrived and it had been about half an hour since our arranged meeting time passed. Finally, Johanna said, "I'm going to go see if I can contact a Pallentinian on the mainland and ask about him." Then she walked out. We all waited in silence for her return.

Suddenly, she busted in screaming, "War has broken out on the mainland. Let us move!"

Malachi yelled, "Johanna! Stop!" He took a deep breath after she froze, then said, "We are king and queen. We cannot go to the front lines ourselves, not for a land that is not our own, especially not while you are with child. That is the heir to the throne of Tendu you are carrying. Don't you understand who you are now, my love? You are no longer a miraculous Pallentinian warrior that battles relentlessly for what she believes in, you are the inspirational Tendu Queen who fights with her wit whenever possible. Now, send word to our troops to leave immediately. Tell them all but what we need to defend ourselves is to go. I will go tell the king here to deploy their troops because knowing Jameson, he is likely in battle. And after you are done, get word to Nollent and Mallishrine too. Kai, Cal, Josie, what you do is your choice. If you choose to go into battle, I will watch Lilly until you return, you have my word that she will remain safe."

Johanna shook her head. "Fine, I will do as you wish. However, I must say that it is you who does not know who I am anymore."

The three of us just looked at each other and sighed, I said, "You guys know I have to go, right?"

Kai said, "We know you do. But we also know that you want us to stay with Lilly, we cannot accept that, though. Take Cal with you, his runes are more powerful than mine. I will stay and care for her. Just promise me that you two will come back, okay?"

Cal nodded. "I promise."

I added, "I promise too."

Then, I looked at Malachi and said, "Tell the King of Oceanica that Cal and I will be leaving with his troops."

Malachi nodded and said to me, "Josie, you are strong but please, remember you have people who love you. Be careful out there, okay?"

I nodded. After that, we all made our preparations. I explained to Lilly, "Look, Cal and I have to go away for a little while. There are some people who need our help right now, but I promise, I will come back for you."

She replied, "You already saved me, go save the rest of the world now, Josie. I understand that I am not the only one who needs you. Kai will take good care of me."

I smiled and hugged her. Then looked at Kai and said, "I love you."

He nodded. "I love you too, Josie. Go be a hero. We will be okay until you get back."

Then I took Cal's hand and we ran off toward the docks. Malachi walked up to Kai after we were out of sight and said, "They'll be okay."

Kai replied, "It just sucks, you know? We came all this way and we are still fighting. Did we really change the world?"

Malachi replied, "We changed our world. It is definitely a good start, isn't it? If this had happened before, Josie would have been on the mainland with her family, a powerless little noble girl subject to the violence of war, and the mainland would have fallen. Now, she is a fearsome priestess with the power to save them all and they have so many allies, other allies coming to help as well. I doubt that they will lose. Though, I am sure this war will not be easily won either, the cost of war is never cheap…."

Kai forced himself to smile through his tears. "Yes, she is far from powerless nowadays…."

Then, Johanna came to give a report. "Everyone's troops have deployed. They will keep us updated as much as they can. We should head home, Oceanica has a king to care for it, Tendu will need us."

Malachi replied, "I agree, are you coming, Kai, Lilly?"

Kai nodded and they all headed back to Tendu as we headed for battle.

We all knew this war had just begun. We all knew that lives would be lost. What we did not know is how soon we would lose one of our own. No sooner did Cal and I arrive than I was getting a report from a general and an attack was launched that I did not see coming. Before it could hit me, Cal jumped in the way. He died immediately. I fell to my knees at his side and screamed, "Cal! Cal! Oh, no. What have they done to you? Wake up! Please, wake up! Cal!" The general tried to get me to run with him and leave Cal's body as a barrage of violent attacks was hitting us, but I could not bring myself to do it.

In that moment, my emotions spiraled out of control because of my grief. I was lifted from the ground by the mass of spiritual energy I accumulated around mine and Cal's bodies to prevent any further damage being done. As we floated in midair, I said, "How dare you take him from me? You will come to rue this day for all eternity." Then, I thrust my arms out as I spun in a circle, releasing all the spiritual energy I had at once, creating a targeted spirit explosion that took out every enemy soldier within ten miles of me, but did not harm friendly men, hundreds died immediately.

Jameson recognized my power and came to me, realizing what had happened when he arrived, he said to me, "I am sorry for your loss. I understand you are grieving, but this is war, Josie. We need you. Can you grieve after, please?"

I stood up with an expressionless look on my face, I said to the general that I had been speaking to previously, "Send word to Kai and get Cal's body back to him. I am going to join the front line."

Jameson turned to the general and said, "You heard the lady, do as you were told."

It was clear the general was terrified of me and he scrambled to do as I said. When I reached the front lines, the battle really started. Jameson stood by me and said, "My wife is safe in the palace. I will honor Cal's final wish to protect you and fight by your side until this is over."

I replied, "I do not know why he did it, that attack would not have killed me. I am far more powerful now."

Jameson smiled a little. "My guess? That was not a factor in his mind. It was not worth the risk to him. In that moment, he likely only saw your life or his. He was not thinking logically, he was simply a man in love. It is what any man in love would have done." With tears running down my face, I fought with Jameson at my side. I was grateful to have a friend like him at a time like this. It is thanks to him I was able to keep fighting. It is thanks to him that my grief did not consume me. I appreciated that more than I ever told him.

Meanwhile, back in Tendu, Kai, Malachi, and Johanna had just received word of Cal's death and that his body would be arriving within a week. Kai was ruined. He left Lilly in Malachi and Johanna's care while he vanished. Malachi waited a few days, assuming he would resurface after he calmed down some, but he did not. Eventually, Malachi became worried and sent out a search party. Johanna asked, "Will you notify Josie?"

Malachi shook his head. "Not until I have a better idea of what is going on. This is not what she needs to hear while she is grieving in the middle of a war."

Johanna nodded. "You are right. She should have a clear mind. Whatever that means in a situation like this."

Malachi asked Johanna, "What do we do now?"

Johanna replied, "I guess we wait. Isn't that all we can do?"

Malachi grumbled. He was not big on waiting. He felt helpless, as if the world were tumbling down around him and he was only able to sit and watch. He had quickly grown weary of being king. He missed just being Malachi, the guy who always did what he felt was right in the moment. No one could blame him for feeling that way. He had given up his freedom, his ability to help his friends in crisis, and much more in the name of peace that was being threatened by a new enemy that he could not even go confront.

Back on the mainland, Jameson and I were stuck in a deadlock with the enemy. We were stronger, but their numbers were great and they were willing to die. We realized that we would run out of energy before they ran out of men. We needed backup. The other troops were tied up in their own battles, but there was a Pallentinian messenger boy nearby. I called out to him, "You, Pallentinian, send a message for me: 'Malachi, Johanna, king and queen though you may be, you are warriors as I am priestess, in your blood. Jameson and I are not well, if you do not come, we may not live. So, I call on you in my hour of need knowing in my heart that you will not forsake me, my dearest friends.'"

The messenger went to send the message immediately. Then Jameson said, "It'll take them almost a week to get here."

I replied, "And?"

He asked, "What are we going to do right now?"

I answered, "Wait. Isn't that all we can do?"

He asked again, "Yes, but can we hold out that long?"

I asked sarcastically, "Do you have another option I am unaware of?"

He laughed and said, "I guess not."

Meanwhile, unbeknownst to all of us, Kai was in a bar in a remote area of Tendu. The bartender asked him, "Young man, you've been in here for days, what's wrong?"

Kai replied, "I lost one of my loved ones."

The bartender was empathetic, "Well, I'm sorry to hear that, my wife died about a year ago."

Kai asked, "What did you do?"

The bartender smiled gently. "I waited for the wound to heal. What else could I do?"

Kai scoffed and left the bar mumbling, "I know exactly what I'll do."

He went to a mountain cliff and began yelling to himself, "Wait for it to heal? How could I? Cal has always been there; it will never heal! How can I ever love her again when he would have never been in that war if she had not gone? How can I love her again when he would not be dead if he had not tried to protect her? How can I love myself again when I told him to go? I cannot! I cannot do this! I am sorry." Kai's grief was more than he could bare. He felt he had no option but to end his own life. I regret not leaving the war and returning to Tendu to help him through it. That day, with tears rolling down his face, he threw himself from the cliff and drowned in the water as he drowned in his sorrows.

His body was found within a few days and Malachi was notified. They also received my message earlier that day. Johanna said to Malachi, "One of us should go tell her."

Malachi sighed. "I will go. Stay here with Lilly."

Johanna understood why it had to be Malachi to go, even though she wanted to. She understood that I would need him at my side when I heard this horrific news. She nodded with fear in her heart and said, "I won't say goodbye to you."

Malachi smiled. "I would expect nothing less, you are indeed my warrior queen. I apologize for not seeing that you needed to be both or that Tendu needed you to be both. I love you, Johanna." And then she watched him depart as she fought to hold back the tears that were so desperately attempting to come out of her eyes. When he was out of sight, she finally released them from their cage and cried briefly. Once she regained her composure, she stood proud as she felt confidence that he would return to her safely swell up inside her.

A week later, Malachi arrived in Loft and found me. Jameson and I were exhausted when he did. He waited to tell me until we broke free of the deadlock we had been stuck in for nearly a week. Malachi was at full energy, so it ended quickly when he released his flames. He had become more powerful after receiving the rune blessing as King of Tendu. He took us to get medical attention after that. We were both injured and extremely fatigued. Once I regained my consciousness fully, he told me about Kai. Unable to process what I was being told, I just nodded. This time was different, I felt something in me break. I had lost Kimble, Cal, and Kai now. I was devastated.

In that moment, I remember the words the Pallentinian Chief spoke to me so long ago. He said, "That longing will either destroy you or save them, it's a thin line, I advise you to walk it carefully." I wondered how he knew. I wondered what I did wrong, what we did to make our longing cross the line? Why didn't I save them? Why did our love destroy me?

At first, my depression took the form of rage. Which was convenient due to the war that was still raging in Loft. I blacked out. I do not remember anything that occurred for the next four days. When I came to, I was standing in the center of a battlefield completely drained of energy. Apparently, Malachi and Jameson had been chasing me trying to stop my rampage, so they were nearby. They would not give me the details of what I had done. When I asked, both looked away. Malachi said to me, "Josie, it may be best if you don't know exactly what happened."

Jameson forced a smile as he said, "Yes, the important thing is that the three of us are safe. And we won the war, thanks to you. You did brilliantly, Josie. You helped save Loft from an invasion."

Malachi nodded. I sighed, fearing that I had become a monster in my emotional rampage. Even in war, killing out of anger is not right. I need to learn to control my emotions better. With power like mine, if I ever fully lost control, who knows what I could do?

16

After that, I returned home to Lilly. She was elated to see me, and I was to see her as well. We all gathered to hold a proper burial for Kai and Cal. Lilly was still young, so I struggled to explain to her what had happened. Talking about these things is never easy, but I guess it is necessary. After all, if an issue is never dealt with it insists on becoming bigger until you acknowledge it. It was strange in the house, not having them around. It was strange everywhere. New representatives were appointed to our team, which was weird too. The Chief came to the funeral as well, to pay his respects to the boys. He never met them, but they fought for peace. He felt that they deserved to be honored properly for it.

I pulled him aside after the service and said to him, "You once told me that the love the three of us had would either destroy me or save them, I have to ask you this now—"

He interjected, "Josie, I know what you intend to ask me. Young priestess, I cannot give you the answers you seek. You must find them for yourself. You are more than capable. All I can tell you is that the line is still being walked."

I asked, "What do you mean by that, though? Are you telling me I can still save them? How, though? I do not understand."

He replied, "I can say no more about the matter, Josie. I am sure you will find the answers, though you may not find them here. Good luck, Priestess Josella Marie Spade Lucietta III, may your travels be safe ones."

I had no clue what he was talking about, but he walked away without explaining. I guess, I would find out in time. Hopefully, I would make the right decisions along the way. At that moment, I decided it was best I just return to the house and talk to Lilly, who had headed back with Johanna.

When I arrived, I thanked Johanna for taking her home and waiting with her, then she left. I said to Lilly, "Hey, pretty little lady. Do you understand what happened to Kai and Cal?"

She shook her head. I sighed and explained, "Well, sometimes when you love someone, you try really, really hard to protect them from people that would hurt them. And Cal loved me a lot, so when he tried to protect me, the people hurt him instead. Then, Kai found what happened and since Kai loved Cal a whole lot, it really hurt him to hear that Cal was gone. Now, Kai could have let any of us know that he needed help to get through this, but Kai did not see that option. The only option he saw was to go away like Cal did, so that they could be together."

Lilly began crying, "But didn't Kai love us too? And didn't you love Cal, why didn't you protect him?"

I knew she was just a child asking questions, but her words cut deep. I said to her, "I wanted to protect Cal, I tried to, but I failed. I did love him, though. I loved them both. As for Kai, of course he loved us, but he was hurt and when you are hurt, sometimes you make decisions you cannot take back. That is why I want you to know that when you are hurt, no matter what the situation is, you can always talk to me about it. You can talk to your uncle Malachi and aunt Johanna too, even Jameson, whoever you want. Just pick an adult you trust and we will help you find a better way of dealing with the pain."

Lilly replied, "Then, Josie, I should probably tell you that even though I understand why they are gone. I am hurt right now, and I am angry too."

I hugged her and said, "Me too, baby girl. Why don't we work through the pain together?"

She nodded as she hugged me back.

Moving on after that was hard, but I did my best. I asked Johanna one day, "Johanna, after all the effort I gave to make the world a place where everyone could be happy, didn't I deserve to be happy? I mean, look at all I lost giving my all to everyone else?"

Johanna smiled gently. "Josie, look at all you found. You never would have met Kimble, Kai, or Cal. Hell, you never would have met me or Malachi, or Jameson for that matter. You never would have found your own power and strength. I know you are hurting right now, but you must remember you still came out of this with far more than you started with. Plus, you will find love again. Maybe not right away, but in time."

I sighed. "You're right, I guess."

Then, we just stared into the sky. Suddenly, Lilly came running out and said, "Josie, look…."

She closed her eyes for a moment and this small fox appeared on her shoulder. I said to it, "Hello there, what is your name?"

The fox replied, "Hi, Josie, I am Kimella. My mom told me to tell you she said 'hello, old friend, keep your head up.' My mom's name is Kimble, by the way."

I began laughing uncontrollably, yet crying at the same time, and said, "How ironic? Of course, her connection would be with your daughter!" Then I calmed down and smiled, still crying, and said, "Kimella, huh? Wonder where she got that one? Tell your mom I said, 'Thank you.' And you two have fun playing." Then I petted her and patted Lilly's head.

I turned back to Johanna and she smiled at me. Neither of us spoke, but much was said at that moment. It was the first time in months that I felt okay. A tiny bit of hope leaked back into my heart and somehow, I knew it would continue to grow. Kimella, meaning Kimble and Josella, that way we would always be together. I suddenly began to wonder, my ancestor, the priestess who fought for the mainland in the war, was her familiar from Kimble's line? I was almost willing to bet it was.

A few days later, Johanna went into labor. Malachi was freaking out when I arrived, pacing up and down the hall. I asked him, "Malachi, who's in there with her?"

He answered, "The healer is, of course."

I replied, "You fool!" and rushed into her. I got the distinct impression he did not know what he did wrong. It did not take long until the baby was born. It was a boy. I looked out into the hall and said, "Get in here and meet your son, Malachi."

He ran in and said, "Oh my, it is a boy. It is a prince."

Johanna asked, "What will we name him?"

Malachi smiled and said, "I think Michael James Tendu is nice."

Johanna replied, "I like that. Michael James, it is." Then she said to me, "Oh, Josie, we had a question for you?"

I nodded. Then Malachi said, "Will you be his godmother?"

I smiled and said, "Yes, of course. I will always be here for you guys." I was enjoying playing with the baby boy, Michael was adorable. He looked a lot like Malachi, honestly.

The days continued to pass and life carried on. One day, Malachi called me to the palace. When I arrived, I asked, "What is it?"

He explained, "Josie, I need you to go to the mainland and meet with Jameson, Sonya, and a diplomat from the Kingdom of Rallem."

I asked, "Rallem? Rallem is far inland? There are five kingdoms in between Loft and them."

He sighed. "Yes, but word of your power has spread and it is causing some issues. They wish to know that you are not a threat to them."

I nodded. "Watch Lilly for me. I will send word to keep you up-to-date."

Malachi laughed as I grumbled and moaned, "There's a ship waiting for you at the docks."

With that, I left for Loft, again. Upon arrival, Jameson met me. He took me to the palace and gave me chambers to settle into. He explained, "I get the impression this may be a long visit, peaceful in nature, but long. I suggest you get comfortable. I understand a lengthy visit is unexpected so if you need anything, please let me know. We are prepared to accommodate you in any way possible. The first meeting is tomorrow morning so feel free to do as you wish until then."

I replied, "Thank you, Jameson, but can we not with the formalities? We are friends. Can we just talk and catch up? I kind of missed you."

Jameson sighed. "That is a relief. I was not sure if it would be awkward for you. I mean, we have not really talked in months. I missed you too! Come on, I know a place we can go to relax some away from the stuffy atmosphere here."

I nodded and followed him. He led me out of the palace through a hole in the gates around the gardens and up a small mountain, then through a tunnel in the side of it. As we crossed through it, I asked, "Jameson, where the hell are we going?"

He laughed. "You'll know when we get there, trust me."

I sighed. "In the meantime, tell me about your runes then. I just realized yours are the only ones I still do not know."

"First, you have Lagu, spirituality, safe haven, water. Next, Ansuz for divine inspiration, the Gods, and speech. Lastly, Nyd for necessity."

I nodded; those runes fit him well.

When we came out the other side of the tunnel, we were on the seaside half of the mountain. Beautiful, green grass and flowers were all up the side of it. I looked out and said, "Oh my, Jameson, this is gorgeous."

He replied, "I know. I found this place a while back and I come out here whenever I want to get away."

I asked, "What are you trying to escape? You are a prince by blood, not just marriage. You are used to the duties."

He sighed. "Sonya is not exactly the easiest person to be married to if I'm being honest."

I nodded. "I understand. I will not pry, but if you want to talk about it, I am here." I began to think about the sacrifice he made for our cause back then. I wondered how much we all lost in our fight to do what was right. Malachi lost his freedom; he was always so adventurous and now he is stuck in the palace almost all the time. Johanna lost her home and her culture; she has not been to Pallentine since she left and she must conform to the ways of the Tendu Kingdom that she rules. Jameson lost his chance at love, agreeing to an arranged marriage. Kai and Cal lost their lives, and I lost them as a result. Lilly lost two fathers after she had already lost her biological parents due to their unfair views. I wondered if we would ever find a way to take back our happiness.

Jameson noticed that I was in deep thought and said, "We have all lost so much. Don't you think it is unfair? Maybe, we should try to take back some of what we lost? The two of us, together?"

I asked, "What are you proposing?"

He explained, "After we finish up business, let's take an 'us day,' we deserve a break."

I laughed a little. "What do you suppose we do on this 'us day'?"

He answered, "Whatever we want, that's the whole point."

I shook my head. "Jameson, you know we cannot do that…. As nice as it sounds, one day is not going to fix this mess we have made of our lives. We must find something bigger, something that will bring us joy in the long run. That is what we deserve."

He smiled. "Always so wise, Josie. You are right. Let us promise each other we will find it, then."

And so, we promised, then we went back to the palace. The following day, we had the meeting with the diplomat. When I entered the room, Jameson was already there, so was the diplomat. He was a handsome man. He was tall and he had the build of a god. He had long, wild hair and his eyes were like gold. He had no runes symbols, but he had some other strange markings on his arms. His smile was nice too. I would not deny that he was an attractive man.

I sat down and said, "Hello, I am Josella, but you can call me Josie. I understand that your kingdom has some concerns about my power."

He replied, "Not so much about your power, but about how it will be used. My king fears your allies will use it to mobilize an attack against our kingdom."

I laughed hysterically. "No offense, sir, but you are hilarious. My allies cannot use my power, only I can use it, and I only deploy when I deem it appropriate to do so. If you spoke to me like a human being instead of a weapon, you may soon realize that I would never deploy such an attack. The rumors you have heard began because I used my spiritual power to DEFEND my ally from an invasion. I assume that your king has selected a diplomat competent enough to understand that, correct?"

"You are certainly not one to be treated as a doormat," he replied. "I will be glad to relay that message to my king. It is clear that no one will be using you for anything." Then he said to Jameson, "Prince Jameson, I apologize, it would seem our concerns about your friend here were quite unwarranted. I must ask, though, would the two of you be interested in discussing a few other matters during my time here? One way or another we will be spending the next month or so meeting with each other. Perhaps we can open trade routes between our lands, or even create a new alliance?"

Jameson looked over at me as if he were waiting for me to answer. I think that he was letting me take charge because I intimidated him when I got irritated. So, I answered, "We can certainly discuss such matters, but just so we are all clear, there will be no agreement unless I give the word. The King and Queen of Tendu, the Chief of Pallentine, and the Prince of Oceanica are all my close friends, and the king and queen of this land are my cousins, I am also revered on Mallishrine for my spiritual prowess. If I am against you, no one will support you. I would suggest transparency and friendliness be your strategy going forward, rather than hairbrained accusations. That is how these alliances were created and that is how any further alliances will be decided."

He nodded hesitantly, then said, "Pastel."

I asked, "What?"

He explained, "I apologize, I never even bothered to introduce myself. Please, do not allow my unruly behavior to shape your view of my kingdom or my king. My name is Pastel."

I laughed. "Pastel, great. You do know that you are a diplomat, right? It is your job to behave in a way that represents your kingdom and your king."

He replied, "No, I am a prince. It is my job to learn the responsibilities that come with being a diplomat so that when I am king and choose my own, I might choose wisely the man that will represent my kingdom. Fortunately, I have a wise priestess that might be able to help me along the way."

I shook my head. "Prince? You cannot be? You are the prince my parents intended for me to wed when I left home?" I scoffed. "I suppose that is irrelevant now. You will need all the help you can get if you are to learn the first thing about diplomacy. Perhaps you should begin with trying to get along with us. This alliance has been built on friendship."

He smirked. "Yes, I am. It is a pleasure to finally meet you, Josie. It seems that after running away from our engagement, you had quite the journey. You are even more desirable as a bride now than you were originally. Trust me when I say, I want nothing more than to get along with you."

I scoffed and walked out; Jameson followed behind me swiftly, attempting to hide the shock on his face. When we got far enough away, he said to me, "Josie! You like him?"

I replied, "No, I do not. He is both rude and entitled; the two do not make for a good combination. I mean, you saw how he behaved, right? It is as if he wants to provoke me into attacking."

He giggled. "I can still feel the sexual tension, Josie, there's no use in lying."

I scoffed, "No, Jameson. He is certainly an attractive man, but do you know what else he is…? An ass."

Jameson became hysterical. "Of course! That is why you like him. Josie, we said something big, right? This is big, it is colossal, in fact. I am not saying to marry the man tomorrow, I am just saying to keep your mind open to the possibilities as we keep meeting with him. As he said, we have a month one way or another."

I sighed. "Look, James, I am not interested. Listen, I think I can still save Kai and Cal; I was not going to tell anyone. I am only telling you because it is easier, so please keep it quiet?"

He answered, "Oh, jeez. How is that possible? I do not understand."

I explained, "I am not sure yet, I am still finding answers myself. But it might be, so I need you to trust me."

He nodded. "I get it. You must try if you think there is even the slightest possibility, but do not close your heart or mind off, okay? We made a promise."

I nodded in agreement, then we were on our way. For the next month, I would be right back where I started, on the mainland, in Loft. The prince and I were starting to get along rather well. I was trying to be open to the possibilities, not just ones between Prince Pastel and me, but anything that may come, especially if I felt they might lead to answers about Kai and Cal. I felt more hopeful than I had in a long time. I decided that I would try to make the best of this situation and try to enjoy it. I figured that a lot was going to happen in the near future, so I may as well try to get something positive out of it. I also enjoyed reflecting on all that had happened already, though. I was proud of who I had become.

There was much for me to be proud of. I had gone from a ridiculously spoiled noble with no regard for others to a proud, kind, and loving priestess that was revered, respected, and loved by so many. I had made friends, improved upon myself, and helped so many on my journey. When I ended the war, it was estimated that about ten thousand Loftian lives were saved because I ended it so quickly.

When the following day came and it was time for our meeting, I walked in and immediately recommended that we skip having a formal meeting that day and just go and have fun. I figured that since the goal was to become friends, it was a clever idea. Neither Pastel nor Jameson objected to it, so we went forward with it. We decided we would give Pastel a tour of all the best spots in Loft. It was going to be an exciting day. Honestly, I had no clue what was going to happen next, but I knew that it was going to be interesting.

As we were leaving, a messenger stopped me with a letter from Johanna and Lilly. I decided to read it as we walked the halls towards the door. It read:

> *"Dear Josie,*
>
> *I know there has been many unexpected twists and turns in our journey. I also know that some of those twists and turns have caused you unimaginable pain. As you move forward and take these next steps, do so proudly. You are a strong and brilliant woman with so many people who love you. Malachi and I will always be*

here for you so please, do not hesitate to call on us if need be. We are forever on your side. Also, keep in mind that Kai and Cal remain at your side in spirit. I know they would want you to find happiness again. We miss you, Josie. Malachi sends his love too. The next part is from Lilly.

Hey Josie,

I just wanted to tell you to take your time finding whatever you need to find. I am okay here for now and I know you will come back for me soon enough. I love you and miss you. Make sure you take of yourself, okay?"

I smiled at the sweet words they wrote, then a thought hit me. I asked Jameson and Pastel to wait a few minutes for me. I ran off to a place I knew I could be alone. After that, I closed my eyes and I tried to focus. I entered the spirit world. With Johanna's words *"they'll always be with you in spirit,"* I wondered if I could reach a human spirit. It turns out, I could reach human spirits. They appeared before me and Kai immediately began apologizing, "Josie, I am sorry. I left you all alone. I caused you even more pain."

I replied, "Do not apologize to me, Kai. I am not mad at you one bit. I just miss you. I miss you both." I started to cry.

Cal smiled. "Do not cry, Josie. We will always be with you and Lilly. Live your life, we are always going to be with you."

I nodded, not wanting to tell them that I thought I could save them until I was confident. Then, I tried to hug them, but I could not. I forgot they were spirits, not physically materialized. So, I said, "Can we talk a bit?"

They nodded, and we sat together, then Cal said to me, "We were there when you talked to the Chief, Josie. We heard the whole thing. We are not like animal spirits. Even you will not know if a human spirit is nearby unless it wants you to. We should talk about it; you do not need to protect us."

I nodded and said, "There really is not much to talk about yet. I do not know anything. This Prince Pastel guy has odd timing, though the Chief said my answers may not be here. Perhaps they are in his kingdom, Rallem. Maybe I will get the opportunity to go there one day soon. We are discussing an alliance with them apparently."

Kai said, "Well, whatever it is, I trust that you will find the answers and do what is right. And Josie, please be careful. Do not put all your eggs in this basket. Of course we want to come back to you, but if it does not pan out, you need to have other sources of joy."

Cal added, "Also, if you were to fall in love, it would not mean you love us any less. We would not be mad or upset. If moving on is what you decide to do eventually, please know that is okay. Whatever you do will be what is best for everyone."

Kai nodded in agreement, then I said, "I love you guys."

They replied, "We love you too, Josie. You should get going now; your next journey awaits you. Have fun, okay? We are here anytime you want to talk, just let us know."

I nodded and returned to the material world and went back to Jameson and Pastel. We headed off to our day trip around Loft. By the end of the month, we had a new alliance in place and the time had come for Jameson, Pastel, and I to go to Tendu. It was decided that Pastel needed to meet the rest of the team, and that we needed to get to know the new representatives Levi and Julius, from Nollent better as well.

During the meeting, it was made clear that a leader needed to be appointed to our team. I said, "If we need to appoint a definitive leader, it should be Malachi. He was the one that started all this."

Malachi shook his head. "I am sorry, Josie. I must disagree. Since I am king, my duty is to Tendu. Right now, this alliance is good for Tendu, thus I support it. If it were no longer good for my kingdom, though, I would be forced to betray it, though my hope is that it never happens. The same applies to Johanna, Jameson, and Pastel, their loyalties are first to their kingdom. Levi, Julius, and Pastel are both bad choices because they do not have the same trust in them yet as those who have been here longer. You should be the leader of this team, your loyalty is only to the team and the team alone, you are a revered priestess, and people from across all our kingdoms trust you wholeheartedly."

Everyone else seemed to agree, so I said, "I will do it if you guys think I should. Thank you; it is really an honor. I did not know I had become so significant."

Malachi and Johanna laughed, and she said, "You've always kind of led the team, Josie. You chose over half our original members, myself included. You are peacekeeper, housekeeper, chef, warrior, best friend, sister, mother, priestess, and more. To us, you have always been the person we trust the most."

I was shocked. I had not realized it, but she was right. Everyone had always put an awful lot of faith in me, even when I thought I was useless. Suddenly, Pastel interjected, "Honestly, I have no issue with Josie leading the team. In fact, I think she is a perfect fit for the position. However, I must say I think that the team leader should have at least been to all the kingdoms in the alliance, if not the whole team? She cannot care for all the kingdoms in the alliance equally if she has not seen them all."

Malachi shrugged his shoulders and said, "Let's do it, then."

Johanna asked, "Let's do what exactly, Malachi?"

I replied to her, "Let's go to Rallem, of course."

Jameson asked, "All of us?"

I giggled. "Why not?"

Johanna said, "Malachi, we have a kingdom to rule and a child to raise."

Malachi left, "Michael is young enough to be left with a wet nurse and Tendu is doing well. We can leave a regent in charge for a while, Johanna."

She asked, "Josie, what about Lilly?"

I replied, "She is no normal eight-year-old. Lilly has immense spiritual prowess. Her power is perhaps the only thing I have sensed that even compares to my own, besides the head monk of Tendu, who still only carries about half my power. I think it may be good for Lilly to come on this journey."

Johanna asked, "If the head monk carries half, how much does she have?"

I thought for a moment, then said, "It'll probably be three-quarters once she's fully trained."

They were all astonished, but it was true. Lilly was going to be a fearsome priestess once she grew into her potential. I looked forward to seeing her at her strongest. This trip would make for some decent training, and she could learn a lot. There is no better teacher than experience, after all. Besides, I felt it was my responsibility to train someone who could fill my shoes if something were to happen to me. I knew that the next generation would eventually take over and I intended to be prepared for it when the time came.

With that, we were all in agreement. The entire team was going to Rallem. I hoped to find some answers while I was there. The story of our journey was a long one. As I would soon find out. The answers I would get were not necessarily the answers I wanted, and more than Kai and Cal's lives would be at stake on this journey. Luckily, I would have many friends, both new and old, at my side. However, I think that is a story for another time. For now, I must bid you farewell as I have come to find that this old woman could use some rest. As the years have come and gone, it seems my energy has gone with them. I promise I will continue soon, though, my loves.

THE END